"You're my wife and you're staying my wife."

Before she could speak, Matt continued. "And you're damned well not marrying anyone else."

All the concern Lesley had felt for Matt during his captivity vanished. Who did he think he was, charging back unannounced to take over her life? "Says who?" she demanded.

His glance was as belligerent as hers. "Says me."

She glowered at him, furious. Where was the man she'd dreamed would take her in his arms, whisper how he'd missed her and beg her to take him back. "You're the one who walked out," she reminded him, not bothering to refresh his memory about the time he'd refused to see her.

He rocked back on his heels, hands stuck in his pockets. "And now I'm back."

American author **ANNE McALLISTER** majored in Spanish literature, has a master's degree in theology, copyedited textbooks and ghostwrote sermons. She might never have pursued her earlier interest in writing if a friend hadn't challenged her to write a Harlequin Romance. She has successfully met the challenge with many popular novels in Harlequin's Romance, Presents and American lines. She regards herself as blessed with a "terrifically tolerant husband" and "four opinionated but equally supportive children." In all her stories she writes about relationships—how they grow and how they challenge the people who share them.

Books by Anne McAllister

ANNE McALLISTER

once a hero

Harlequin Books

TORONTO • NEW YORK • LONDON
AMSTERDAM • PARIS • SYDNEY • HAMBURG
STOCKHOLM • ATHENS • TOKYO • MILAN

For Mary Mayer Holmes,
the finest kind of writer and friend.

Harlequin Presents first edition April 1990
ISBN 0-373-11257-2

Original hardcover edition published in 1989
by Mills & Boon Limited

CHAPTER ONE

'A HERO! A reg'lar hero—that's what he is!' Uncle Harry chortled, slapping the bold black headline that proclaimed, 'Hostage Colter Engineers Escape.' 'Who'd a thunk it, eh, girl?'

Lesley, making herself concentrate on ironing the pocket of Teddy's shirt, thought to herself, who wouldn't have? But she didn't say a word. She hadn't ever since she'd heard the news on her way home from work that afternoon. Matt's escape had aroused so many hopes and fears in her that she was still at a loss to sort them all out.

Her participation in the conversation was unnecessary in any case, for Harry went on undaunted, 'Good ol' Matt. Might've known that after fourteen months in that hellhole he'd take things into his own hands. Wonder when he'll get back to the States.' He rubbed his hands together enthusiastically. 'Have to go to Washington probably. At first, anyhow. Debriefings and all that.'

Lesley just nodded.

Harry fixed her with an encouraging smile. 'Suppose you'd better take the kids down to meet him there.'

'No!' That was the one thing she *had* figured out.

The forcefulness of her sudden reply made him blink, and Lesley grimaced. She hadn't meant to sound so adamant, but her confusion made her more determined than ever not to go where she wasn't wanted.

Harry gave her a worried look and backed off a bit, misunderstanding. 'Well, maybe you're right. Matt may have had a rough go of it. Perhaps you ought to ease him into it a bit, and go down there first by yourself . . .'

'I'm—I'm not going either.' Lesley set the iron down and

5

rearranged Teddy's shirt on the ironing-board with great deliberation.

'Not going?' Uncle Harry looked at his great-niece, horrified.

'No, I—can't. I——' But how could she explain the myriad emotions that had assailed her—both joy and panic—at the news that Matt at last was free?

'But you're his wife!' Harry protested.

'The wife he walked out on!'

'Good Godfrey, girl, you're not still frettin' about that, are you? It was his job. He had a story to do. Beirut wasn't it?'

'Bali,' Lesley corrected tightly. 'That time. But it wasn't just the story.'

It had been the whole marriage. Matt had never loved her the way she loved him. If he had, he would have welcomed her with open arms, not refused to see her, not sent the message that he didn't need her any longer in his life.

Of course she was happy he'd escaped captivity. What woman who still loved a man wouldn't be? But to go to him? Seek him out?

She couldn't. It had been two and half years since they had parted, and in that time he'd never given any indication of wanting her back. She didn't imagine that even fourteen months in Middle Eastern captivity would have changed his mind about that. So what point was there in going to see him? She didn't need that kind of rejection again.

Now, if he came seeking her . . .

But she didn't let herself think long about that.

'You really don't want to go?' Uncle Harry looked at her, his pale blue eyes disbelieving behind the wire-rimmed spectacles he wore. He stared at the slender young woman who was his great-niece as if she didn't have the brains that God gave geese.

Lesley bent her head, knowing what he was

thinking, determined to focus on the shirt, not her uncle. 'Why rake up the past?'

'Because you might have a future.' He spoke with more hope than confidence now.

She shook her head, finished the shirt and hung it on a hanger. 'With Jacques, perhaps,' she said more to distract than because she meant it.

Harry's gaze jerked up sharply and he looked at her as if she had gone mad. 'Are you serious?'

'Why not?' Lesley met his gaze stubbornly. 'Jacques Dubois is a wonderful man—steady, secure, stable. And he wants to marry me.'

'He's a lobsterman.'

Lesley gave a half-laugh. 'Is that prejudice or is that prejudice?'

Harry looked affronted. 'I just meant, would a lobsterman make you happy?'

Lesley's smile faded and her expression grew serious as she met Harry's gaze. 'Did Matt make me happy?'

There was a long silence. Finally Harry sighed, then paused and scratched his bald head. 'I thought he did. Didn't he?' he asked eagerly. 'For a while, at least. Seemed to me he swept you off your feet. The way the two of you were those first few weeks——' he smiled, reminiscing, eyes alight '—it was like a fairy-tale come to life.'

But Lesley wouldn't let herself reminisce. The memories hurt too much. She shook her short brown hair away from her face and picked up another shirt, spreading it on the ironing-board. 'Like Cinderella and the prince, you mean?'

'Exactly.'

She grimaced. 'Yes, well, unfortunately the clock waited to strike midnight until after we'd got married.'

Uncle Harry gazed at his niece sadly, taking in the stubborn chin and wide, unsmiling mouth, the sad hazel eyes that had far more hurt in them than one so young should bear. He shook his head. 'Ah, my dear,' he murmured.

Then he looked down again at the newspaper in his hand, at the big bold headlines and the front page article about Matthew Colter, kidnapped foreign correspondent and, now, returning hero. 'A hero ought to have a wife to come home to,' he said firmly.

'Not this one,' Lesley said, and smoothed the shirtsleeve over the ironing-board.

Once upon a time she had worn her heart on her sleeve where Matt Colter was concerned. Now she knew better. If he came to her—if things had really changed—well, that was one thing. But she had no intention of deliberately seeking him out and letting him scorch it again.

The world around Day's Harbor, Maine, where Lesley Colter lived, worked and kept house for Uncle Harry, remembered very quickly whose wife she was. Everywhere she went over the next couple of weeks people wanted to know what she had heard from Matt.

She hadn't.

Hours went by, then days, then a week, then two. But Lesley heard no word. Not that she expected to, of course, she told everyone with a blithe smile that belied the hollow ache she felt within. He had no real obligation to her now, hadn't for years really, though they had never divorced.

Anyway, she knew from prior experience that Matt operated with 'big picture' mentality. How events affected particular individuals didn't interest him. She doubted that he had any idea that his disappearance and subsequent captivity had affected her at all. If he even gave her a thought, Lesley guessed that he would expect her to read in the papers that he had escaped, and that, though wounded, he was all right.

And that, she was sure he would conclude, would be enough for her.

It was, she told herself as time wore on without any word from him at all. And she did everything in her power to convince herself that it was true.

Matt's escape was not, however, the nine days' wonder Lesley had hoped it might be. Though she did not hear from him directly, she seemed unable to escape him. He was on the front pages of all the papers, in the lead stories of all the newscasts, on the covers of *People*, *Time*, *Newsweek*, even *Rolling Stone*.

Any day now, Lesley told herself, the world, curiosity sated, would move on to worthier topics. But she was wrong.

The world, war-weary and worn, fed up with the increasing erosion of public safety at the hands of terrorists, was delighted to have a new hero and reluctant to relinquish him. They loved Matt Colter, though he did little, oddly enough, to encourage their enthusiasm for him.

Perhaps, Lesley thought, if he had been balding like Hobart, chinless like Luther or over sixty like Griswald—the other three men whose escape to safety he'd masterminded along with his own—they would have let him go more readily. But lean, handsome, daring men who risked their lives to outwit terrorists were not thick on the ground.

The world was enchanted with Matt Colter. It couldn't get enough of him.

Lesley almost went mad.

It would have been nice if he'd called simply so she could have said to people, 'Yes, we talked. No, he's not coming around. We always intended to go our own separate ways, and now we can.'

But he didn't. And Lesley waffled along in a limbo of her own making until her mother, of all people, shook her out of it.

Madge Fuller had spent her life being blown this way and that by the winds of fate and the comings and goings of her ne'er-do-well husband Jack. She was an example of exactly the sort of woman Lesley didn't want to become, and her marriage had been exactly the sort of marriage that Lesley had been determined hers would never be. So it came as a

bit of a shock to have Madge sit right there in the front
room, take one look at Lesley's pale, thin face and lacklustre
smile, and say, 'You're just like me.'

Lesley's head jerked up from her contemplation of a
basket of laundry to stare at her mother's tired, worn face.
'What do you mean?'

'You're missing him dreadfully. Can't live without 'im.'

'I——'

'Exactly the way I was missing Jack.'

'I——'

'I was waiting and waiting, just the way you are,' her
mother went on, a sad, dreamy look on her face that set
Lesley's teeth on edge. 'Always was. Then he'd come home
and . . .' She gave a vague wave of her hand.

'Leave again,' Lesley finished for her mother, snapping
the towel she was folding and thumping it on the pile. 'It's
not the same, Mom.'

But Madge just shook her head. ''Course it is. Happens
like that with us. Waitin' . . . hopin' . . .'

Never making a move on our own, Lesley thought. She
shook her head, refusing to accept it. She had always hated
the aimlessness she had seen in her mother, the lack of
ability to take charge of her own destiny, the failure to take
any positive steps to make something out of her life. And
Madge saw the same thing in her? Good Godfrey! as Uncle
Harry would have said.

Madge left half an hour later, but her words lingered long
after, haunting Lesley, taunting her. Was she simply going
to dither around forever like her mother because Matt did
not call her? Was she too much of a ninny to grasp the reins
of her own life and make something of it?

Of course she wasn't!

She was certain he wasn't sitting around twiddling his
thumbs waiting for her. He'd be getting on with his life
now. Probably he was half-way to Afghanistan already. It
was time, she told herself smartly, that she got on with hers.

Jacques agreed with her.

He was sitting in the kitchen on a rainy Saturday morning in May listening to Lesley mutter on about what Madge had said the day before. They were alone, the children being at friends' houses and Harry having gone to the dentist. Lesley kneaded the dough for cinnamon rolls, thumping the daylights out of it, taking out on it all the aggression she hadn't taken out on her mother. And when she had finished he nodded his head and said, 'So let's get married.'

Lesley gulped, her hands strangling the dough. 'Well, I . . .' She faltered for a moment.

'He's back safe, right?'

'Yes,' slowly.

'You didn't feel right divorcing a man in his situation, right?' He gave her an enquiring look.

She had said that. 'Yes.'

'So . . . his situation has changed. And now you say you want to change yours. So . . .' Jacques spread his hands, a look of hopeful expectancy on his handsome Gallic face.

'So . . .' Lesley shrugged awkwardly, squeezing the dough between her fingers. So. So? she asked herself. So? What was she waiting for?

The phone call? It wasn't going to come now, and she knew it. Her fantasy of Matt arriving on her doorstep, contrite and loving, was just that—a fantasy. It bore no more relationship to real life than she bore to the Queen of Sheba.

What *was* she waiting for?

Matt Colter's blessing? Fat chance.

He had probably forgotten she was even alive. Jacques was right: she had stalled about the divorce long enough. She had no more excuses. It was crazy even to think about hanging on.

She would do far better with Jacques. He loved her—had loved her for years. He was strong and calm and dependable, like the clear, steady beam from a lighthouse in the stormy sea of her life. And in her way Lesley loved him, too. It would never be with the thunderous passion and intensity with which she had loved Matt. But so what? Were thunder and stormswept seas all that enticing? Not to a woman who had been dashed on to a rock-strewn coast.

Divorce Matt? Yes. But that was simply burying something long dead that she hadn't admitted to herself had died. She needed to do more than that. She needed to do something positive.

She looked hard at Jacques and found him looking equally seriously back at her. It wasn't the first time he had asked her. It wasn't the first time she had considered accepting. It was, however, the first time that she managed a tremulous smile and a slightly croaky, 'Yes.'

Jacques, who must have been holding his breath throughout this entire deliberation, let it all out in a whoosh, wrapped his arms around her and swung her round and round the kitchen. 'Thank heaven,' he muttered, burying his face in her short brown hair. 'At last! I almost don't believe it!' He set her back on the floor, closed his eyes and kissed her soundly on the mouth.

The screen door banged behind them.

'Congratulate me, Harry!' Jacques swung round, beaming. 'I'm going to get married.'

'Not to my wife,' a rough baritone countered, and Lesley grabbed the countertop for support.

'*Matt!*'

'Colter?' The animation in Jacques' voice died.

They both stared at the lean, dark man holding on to the door-jamb with one hand and with a duffel bag in the other, a bitterly sardonic smile on his face as he nodded. 'At your service.'

Then he turned to Lesley and gave her a narrow look. 'Did you divorce me?' he demanded.

'Not . . . exactly.' She licked her lips, still stunned at the sight of him, wondering what he was doing here after all this time, and why he had come at all when he could only glare at her angrily. 'Not yet.'

'Not, period,' said Matt, his dark eyes gleaming.

Lesley's spine stiffened at his peremptory attitude. 'What do you mean?'

'I mean you're my wife, and you're staying my wife. You're damned well not marrying anyone else.'

All the concern Lesley had felt for him during his captivity vanished in the space of a blink. Who did he think he was, to come charging back in here unannounced and take over her life? Hadn't he learned anything? 'Is that so?' she demanded defensively.

He met her glare with a belligerent one of his own. 'That's so.'

'Says who?'

'Says me.'

She looked at him scornfully. 'After all these years?'

'After all these years,' he mocked.

She glowered at him, furious. Where was the man she'd fantasised about? The one who would take her in his arms and whisper how he had missed her and beg her to take him back in her life? Dream on, she mocked herself.

'You're the one who walked out,' she reminded him archly, not even bothering to refresh his memory about the time he had refused to see her.

He stuck his hands in his pockets and rocked back on his heels. 'And now I'm back.'

'Just like that?' She couldn't believe what she was hearing.

'Did I need to make an appointment?'

'I'm just . . . surprised, that's all.' Which was putting it mildly. 'How long are you staying?'

'Forever,' he said, confounding her. Then, picking his duffel bag up once more, he limped right past her into the front room. The door that separated it from the kitchen slapped shut in Lesley's astonished face.

For a moment she couldn't speak, could scarcely even breathe. Her mouth opened and shut like a fish, but air was a precious commodity.

Then Jacques put a hand on her arm and turned her to face him. 'He can't . . . you won't . . .' A thousand fears were written on his face.

Lesley pulled away from him, breathing again, but still shaken. 'Fall into his arms? Are you kidding?' Her hands were trembling. She stuffed them into the pockets of her slacks. She felt as if the kitchen floor was shifting beneath her feet.

This couldn't be happening, she told herself over and over. It couldn't. But from the front room she could hear the squeak of the sofa's springs as Matt sat down.

'Forever?' mumbled Jacques. 'Is that what he said?'

'That's what he said.'

'But——'

Lesley gave a bitter laugh. 'But I don't believe it.' She wouldn't let herself. It was a perverse joke. A horrible example of the divine sense of humour at her expense.

'Why'd he come back, then?'

'To drive me crazy—I don't know.' Lesley prowled around the kitchen like a tiger with toothache. 'Maybe he just remembered I'm alive. Maybe somebody reminded him. Maybe,' she said with a half-laugh, 'he heard about Teddy and Rita.'

Jacques winced. 'I'd forgotten about that. He really doesn't know?'

'Not unless someone told him. And I don't know anyone who could.'

Jacques shook his head, smiling grimly at the revelations Matt Colter had in store. 'I'd like to see his face.'

'I wouldn't,' Lesley said, but she would have to, when the time came. She wiped her hands on the sides of her slacks. 'But I have to. And the sooner the better, I think. I—I should go . . . talk to him, Jacques.'

'Want me to stay?'

She shook her head. 'I think this is something we'd better do alone.'

He still looked doubtful. 'You sure?'

She wasn't, but she said she was. Matt had been looking at Jacques with murder in his eye. She didn't want bloodshed on her hands.

Jacques sighed. 'I don't like it.'

She gave his hand a pat that was meant to reassure him, but she needed reassurance as much as he did. 'Nor do I, but it's necessary.'

'He didn't even knock,' Jacques complained.

It wasn't Matt's style to knock. He never had. He came—and went—as he pleased. His behaviour, Lesley thought, was a good indication that he hadn't changed a bit.

'I'll call you later,' she told Jacques.

He still looked reluctant, but when she reached up and gave him a light peck on the cheek he smiled ruefully. 'Promise?'

'I promise,' she said, and watched him shrug into his jacket and go out of the door and down the path. Then, having wiped her hands on the tea-towel she had intended to put over the dough which she still hadn't finished kneading, she took a deep breath, lifted her chin, and walked purposefully into the living-room.

Matt was slouched on the sofa, glaring up at her from burned-out eyes. '"I'll call you later, I promise,"' he mocked her, in a breathy imitation of her own voice.

Lesley's brows shot up. 'You listen at doors now?'

'You hear the most interesting things if you do. Marriage proposals. Promises!' He fairly spat the words.

'I keep mine, at least,' she snapped. 'Anyway, what's it to you?'

'You're my wife!'

'In name, perhaps.'

'A damned good place to start.'

'Why bother?'

He stared at her. 'What are you saying?'

She stood her ground. 'I'm saying I don't know what you're doing here.'

'I came for you.'

'Now?' Disbelief dripped from the word.

'What do you mean, now?' He frowned at her.

'You've been free two weeks. More.'

'I've been "free", as you put it, less than twenty-four hours. I might have got away from Assad and those other bastards two weeks ago, but that doesn't mean I could do anything I pleased the minute I escaped. I was shot, for pity's sake! I was in the hospital in Germany after they flew me out.' He spared a quick glance for his leg. 'I was also debriefed.'

'You're not CIA.'

'Doesn't matter. When the government wants to talk to you, you don't say, sorry, I'd rather not.' He sighed and raked a hand through his hair. 'There was a lot of other stuff. The paper wanted me to do some articles while I was still in governmental clutches . . .'

'Which, of course, you did.'

'Yes, I did,' he said tightly. 'To clear the slate. To come back here. To you.'

One tiny renegade part of Lesley was dying to believe that. But why hadn't he called, at least? 'They have phones,' she said tartly. 'You could have called me.' Her gaze locked with his, challenging him.

Matt met her gaze unflinchingly. 'No, I couldn't.'

'Why not?'

'I had to see you.'

'Why?'

'Why didn't you come to see me?' he countered.

She stared, dumbfounded that he would even ask.

He spread his hands. 'See? Not such an easy question, is it?'

It was easy enough, but in the circumstances she was not going to give him the true answer. Mustering her self-control, she said, 'All right, you're here. Now what?'

'Exactly what I said.'

Lesley shook her head, confused.

'Simple.' He folded his arms behind his head and smiled up at her. And underneath the blandness Lesley heard a hard edge to his voice. 'I'm staying.'

CHAPTER TWO

HE wouldn't, of course. He'd come on a whim, come to stir up her life again, raise her hopes again. And then he would leave her flat. She was sure of it.

It had happened before often enough. She should have guessed what their life would be like before she married him. But she couldn't see beyond the laughing dark eyes that had teased her, beyond the smiles and the kisses and the lovemaking that wooed her. She had been head over heels in love with Matthew Colter, and reality would bend to her wishes, she was certain.

Before the honeymoon was over she had got her first indication that it wouldn't. They had borrowed Uncle Harry's hideaway on Mount Desert Island for their first week of wedded bliss. And, four short days into that week, Becca Walsh, Matt's intense and beautiful colleague at *Worldview*, had appeared at the door.

'All hell is breaking loose in Beirut,' she'd told him, without so much as a glance at Lesley. 'Carlisle wants you out there.'

Lesley had thought Matt would tell Becca Walsh that Carlisle should go to hell, he was entitled to a honeymoon. He had asked what plane he should get on.

Things had gone downhill from there. One word from *Worldview* and their marriage went on hold. Lesley had borne it stoically the first few times, smiling bravely as she waved him off, welcoming him back with apple pie and open arms, telling herself that he needed time to put things in perspective, time to rearrange his values so that their life together came first.

But time hadn't brought solutions. On the contrary, it had brought Becca Walsh more frequently than ever, with

17

her sympathetic cluckings for Matt and her condescending smiles for Lesley. Eventually, once more on Mount Desert Island two and a half years ago, Lesley had had enough.

'Bali,' Becca had said brightly that time, brandishing a plane ticket under Matt's nose, ignoring Lesley, who stood stiffly in the doorway to Uncle Harry's kitchen, her back rigid, her jaw clenched.

Matt had turned to her, clearing his throat, trying to sound apologetic, though Lesley could hear the excitement already threading his voice. It reminded her of the way her father had sounded right before he had upped and left her mother time and time again. 'I've really gotta go, Les. It's important.' Matt had crossed the room and touched her shoulder.

She'd flinched away from him, shaking him off. 'More important than us? You said we'd have a long weekend, Matt. You promised! Two weeks in Bangkok, you said, and then vacation. Time together. Just the two of us.' She glared at him, eyes flashing, not even caring that the demure, sophisticated Becca probably thought she was the world's biggest shrew.

'We've had almost two days,' Matt protested.

Lesley snorted. 'We've had——' she glanced at her watch '—thirty-two hours and twenty-seven minutes.' Less even than Madge had had with Jack.

'They don't plan coups around my schedule,' Matt argued. 'I go where the trouble is, when the trouble is.'

'And to hell with everyone else,' Lesley snapped.

'That's not true.'

'No?'

'No.'

'Then take me with you.'

He stared. 'Be serious!'

'I am. I want time with you. If you can't have it here, I'll go with you there.'

'No way.' He shook his head. She reached for his arm this time, and he shook her off.

'Why not?'

'You could get killed.'

'So could you,' she countered.

'No.'

'You might.'

'I won't.' He scowled at her. He was already packing his duffel bag. 'I'll be fine.'

'You can't guarantee it.'

'I can guarantee I won't if you come with me.'

She blinked. 'What do you mean?'

'I'd be distracted . . . worrying about you.'

'But——'

'No. You're not coming, and that's final.'

'Then don't go.'

'I have to.'

'You don't.'

He shook his head despairingly.

'You want to,' she accused.

'Of course I want to. It's my job.'

'And you love your job more than me, obviously. More than anything, I'd say!'

'I like my work,' he said stubbornly.

'Well, then, *choose* your work,' she flared at him, desperate now, determined not to be the doormat her mother was. 'But you can't have both, Matt. I'm fed up. I'm not a wife, I'm a pit stop. We don't have a marriage! We've got some sort of sexual filling-station where you drop in when your frustration level gets too high!'

Colour flared in his cheeks and he shot a glance at the amused and entertained Becca. 'For heaven's sake, Lesley!'

'You do!' she shouted, grabbing a frying-pan. 'And I've had enough! Go if you want. Get shot if you want. But don't make promises you won't keep. If you leave now, don't come back!'

'Come on, Les,' he cajoled, taking a step towards her, reaching for the pan she brandished. 'She's just a little upset,' he explained to Becca, as if Lesley were his child, not his wife.

'So I gather,' said Becca in a cool, amused tone.

Lesley spun away from him, hating him for his patronising calmness, hating Becca for her smug professionalism, hating the sham their marriage had become. 'I meant it,' she told him coldly, gripping the handle for all she was worth. 'Go if you must. But I don't want to see you again until you're willing to keep the promises you make!'

Their gazes locked in silent combat. Finally Matthew shrugged. 'If that's the way you want it,' he said, with all the nonchalance of a man headed for the corner store. He turned on his heel and walked out.

Lesley flung herself on to the sofa, sobbing, hating Becca, Matt, her mother and father. But most of all hating herself.

Once, several weeks after that, she had gone to his office to see him. Back at college in New York herself, she had hoped he might change his mind and come home when he finished in Bali, willing to rearrange his life. But he hadn't.

After mulling and stewing, Lesley finally decided to go to see him at work. One more chance, she had told herself. Maybe she had over-reacted when her hopes and dreams had been shattered. Maybe she should approach him where he worked, let him see their marriage in that perspective, then try to get him to sit down with her and work things out.

She had been nervous, but determined, all the way up in the elevator. And she knew it was obvious to Becca, who met her just as she was heading down the hall to Matt's office.

'Can I help you?' Becca asked her.

Lesley hesitated. Becca was not a near and dear friend—at least as far as she was concerned. On the contrary, she sometimes found herself envying the other woman's professional association with Matt. But Becca would know where he was. And she probably had a very good idea why Lesley wanted to see him since she had witnessed their last battle, as it were. 'I'm . . . looking for Matt,' Lesley ventured.

'He's in conference with Mr Carlisle right now,' Becca said, nodding at the office across the hall. 'I can see if he's nearly finished.'

'Please.'

'Be right back.' Becca gave her bright smile and vanished behind Dave Carlisle's office door.

Lesley waited, an island of anxiety in the midst of a stream of the harried writers and editors who flowed around her, all preoccupied with events taking place in the far-flung corners of the world and oblivious to whoever was standing right in their midst. It seemed like forever until the door opened again. Lesley drew a deep breath, preparing to begin the short, poignant speech she had prepared to convince Matt that they had to talk things out.

But she never got past the first breath, because it was Becca, not Matt, who shut the door and came to take her arm. 'I don't know what to say.' Becca licked rosy red lips. 'He . . . doesn't want . . . to see you.'

Lesley stared at her, stricken. Becca took her arm and edged her out of the way of a couple of editors talking a mile a minute as they bustled down the corridor.

'I told him you were here,' Becca said apologetically, 'and he just said not to bother him.'

Lesley's lips pressed together in a thin line in an effort to control her pain. Her eyes stung and her throat felt tight. Becca gave her arm a sympathetic squeeze. Lesley blinked fiercely. 'Thank you,' she said softly, 'for trying.'

'You poor dear,' Becca soothed. 'Can I get you something? Coffee? Tea? A brandy? We have some for medicinal purposes, I think.' She cast a glance at the cabinet next to them.

Lesley shook her head and swiped at her eyes. 'No. No, thank you. I . . . I'll just go now.' She knew what Becca thought, and she didn't want the other woman's pity. Before Becca could say another word, Lesley shouldered her way past a chubby man waving a sheaf of papers and bolted out of the door.

Well, if she'd wanted it spelled out for her, it couldn't get any clearer than that, she told herself bitterly as she walked back to the hospital where she was working part-time while she finished her nursing degree. So much for second chances. So much for working things out. So much for fearing that she had over-reacted.

That night she saw a newsclip of several American reporters who were rushing to Central America to cover an assassination attempt and possible coup, and she knew Matt had confirmed once again his priorities. She hadn't misjudged at all.

She hadn't seen him again, except in news photos, until today.

And, now that he was here, what was she going to do with him?

Unable to meet his angry, determined stare, she had taken refuge once more in the kitchen. As she spread the cinnamon mixture on the dough, she tried to make sense of the events of the morning and to decide what to do next.

'Hiding?' The voice behind her made her jump.

She spun around, heart hammering. 'Of course not!'

'Well, the way you bolted out of the living-room——'

'I did not bolt!' she denied hotly.

Matt cocked a doubting eyebrow. 'Looked like it to me. Too bad seeing me again is such a painful experience for you.' His mouth twisted.

'It's not . . . painful,' Lesley lied. Not in the way he meant, at least. 'I was . . . finishing what I'd started.' She indicated the dough on the baking-sheets.

He didn't say anything, just stood watching her for a few moments, and she wondered what he was thinking. Then he prowled around the kitchen, brushing his hand over the counters, peering out of the window towards the harbour, circling her as she worked and tried to pretend that every fibre of her being wasn't standing at attention in awareness of him.

Finally he leaned back against the counter and shook his head. 'I'm surprised you're here.'

Lesley blinked. 'You said you came here looking for me.'

'Because I didn't know where else to start. I figured Harry would know. Might've known you'd be here, though. It's like a time-warp. Everything's just the same, just the way I remembered it. You. This.'

Lesley shook her head. 'No.'

Matt frowned. 'So what's different?' he asked, lifting one hip on to the counter so that the material of his jeans pulled tautly across his thigh. 'You were with Harry and Leila when I met you. You're with Harry and Leila now.'

'Just Harry.'

Matt's head came up with a jerk. 'What?'

'I'm just with Harry. Leila died, Matt. A year and a half ago.'

He looked stricken. His face went even paler than it had been. 'I didn't know. No one said. What happened?'

'Pneumonia. Her heart hadn't been good the last year or so as well. But when it happened, it happened . . . fast. Didn't anyone know how to get hold of you?' she asked.

His jaw tightened. 'You?' he suggested bitterly. Then, as if he had decided that wasn't quite fair, he added, 'I don't know. Probably not.' He raked a hand through his hair, dishevelling it further. 'Poor Leila! Poor Harry.'

'Yes.'

He prowled around the kitchen some more, distracted, raking his fingers through tumbled dark hair. 'At least they had a good marriage,' he said finally.

Lesley gave him a wary look. 'Yes, they did. One of the best.' One she would have liked to have.

What Matt felt, she didn't know. His face reflected a turmoil that surprised her. She supposed it shouldn't have. Harry had been one of his dearest friends, a mentor just leaving the active foreign correspondent's job when Matt was breaking in. And Leila had done her share of mothering

him, Lesley knew. As much as anyone could 'mother' a
man like Matt. Having the news of Leila's death thrust
upon him like this after everything else he had been
through was undoubtedly a blow.

'Cripes,' he muttered under his breath, and she knew he
was still digesting what she had told him. For a long while
he didn't speak again, simply stared out of the window, lost
in thought.

Lesley puttered around the kitchen, made out a grocery
list, unloaded the dishwasher, all the while intensely aware
of the man standing just a few feet from her, yet completely
unsure of what to say.

Finally Matt sighed and perched on the counter, his feet
dangling. 'Any coffee going?'

Lesley nodded.

'Any chance of getting a cup?'

'Certainly.' Glad of something to occupy her, she got a
mug out of the cupboard and filled it with what was left of
the morning's pot. 'I could make you some more,' she
offered. 'This might be too strong.'

He shook his head. 'Doesn't matter. It's fine. A damned
sight better than I've been used to.'

Lesley winced, remembering what he must have been
used to. 'Was it . . . awful?'

Matt's expression grew shuttered. 'Bad enough.' He
eased himself off the counter and moved to the kitchen
table. Once more Lesley noted his limp and the way he
favoured his right leg when he sat, wincing as he adjusted
his jeans. She added a dollop of milk to the mug and carried
it over.

'The papers did say you were wounded. How serious was
it?' she asked him, her eyes going to the area on his thigh
where the jeans stretched tautly over several thicknesses of
bandages.

He shrugged. 'I'll live.' He lifted the mug from where she
had placed it on the table in front of him and carried it to
his lips, drawing in a long breath of steamy coffee-scented

air before shutting his eyes and sipping slowly.

It seemed so normal, so everyday—a wife pouring coffee, a husband drinking it, the two of them just sitting together in companionable silence. Lesley stared at him, entranced at the notion and at how far they were from fulfilling it.

It was the first time she had really looked hard at him since he had walked in through the door. The last two and a half years had aged him considerably. The youthful exuberance which had once lightened his craggy features had all but vanished, and he looked every day of his thirty-four years.

What had once been dimples were now deep grooves in lean cheeks. His forehead was furrowed, and the network of lines that fanned out from the corners of his eyes was far more pronounced than she remembered it. Laughter-lines, she had always thought of them before. Not these. They told of suffering rather than joy.

Matt opened his eyes, swallowed, and looked at her over the top of the mug. 'Thank you,' he said gravely. 'I needed that.' He took another mouthful of coffee, clearly savouring it before letting it trickle down his throat. The fight seemed to have gone out of him. She saw no more anger in his eyes, only weariness and an infinite sort of sadness that made her ache as well. They told her more than all his other features put together, and the story was not a pretty one to tell.

'Can I . . . can I get you anything else?' Lesley twisted the tea-towel in her fingers, needing to do something. 'Are you hungry?'

Matt lifted a shoulder. 'I could eat, I guess.'

'When did you last?'

He shook his head. 'I don't remember. Last night, probably. I think Becca got fried chicken or——'

'Becca?' Lesley felt her heart stop. 'Becca Walsh? You were at Becca Walsh's?' She tried not to let the jealousy she had always felt of the other woman creep into her voice, but she didn't do much of a job of it.

'Since I got out of the hospital I've been at Becca

Walsh's.'

'But——'

'Hotels don't do it when you just get out of the hospital. You're supposed to have someone with you,' he informed her reasonably.

But Lesley didn't feel reasonable. 'But——'

'And as you didn't seem to be there . . .' Matt's mouth twisted as his chin lifted and the fire came back into his eyes.

'You really expected me to be? After what happened between us? After what you did?'

Matt took one last swallow and thumped the mug down on the table. Hauling himself to his feet, he gave her a level look. 'Let's just say, I hoped you might be, considering the circumstances. I guess it was too much to hope for.' He managed a bitter smile. 'I should have realised you'd be otherwise occupied here. I don't think I could eat, after all. Thank you very much.' And he limped out of the room without looking back.

Lesley stared at him, renewed anger and hurt raging within her, battling for primacy. The man was unbelievable! The range of emotions he could evoke in her in the space of a few moments was far greater than those anyone else had elicited in her entire life. He had just spent days in the company of Becca Walsh, and then had the audacity to suggest that he did so only because Lesley wasn't there to care for him when he got out of hospital! As if it were all her fault! As if he hadn't made it perfectly clear he never wanted to see her again!

She slammed her hands down on the countertop, making the toaster jump. Then she picked up his mug and weighed it in her hands. Her fingers itched to heave it at the door that swung shut after him.

Instead she put on her raincoat and let herself out of the back door. A walk in pouring rain would do as much for her frazzled state of mind as breaking coffee-mugs would do. In either case, she didn't think much could be done.

Matt was back, but her dreams certainly hadn't come true. On the contrary, she wasn't sure if the nightmare had not just begun. Whatever his presence meant, things were obviously not going to be the same again.

He was standing at the door an hour later when she came back, and jerked it open as she came up the steps.

'Where have you been?' he asked harshly. He was braced heavily against the doorframe, his dark hair ruffled, the colour high in his cheeks. A feverish glitter lit his dark brown eyes as he glared down at her.

Lesley looked up at him, surprised. 'I went for a walk.' She slipped past him, taking care not to touch him, took off her raincoat and hung it on one of the hooks beside the back door.

'I thought you'd left.' His voice was hoarse, accusatory.

She turned and stared at him, astonished, blinking raindrops from her eyelashes. 'Left? Run away, you mean? I live here.'

'That doesn't mean . . .' His voice trailed off. He rubbed a hand against the nape of his neck, kneading the muscles. 'You didn't say,' he accused finally.

'Isn't that a little strange, coming from the man who was forever walking out of my life?'

'You hadn't just come back from a hellhole, for heaven's sake!'

'No,' she admitted, seeing suddenly that his concern was real. 'I went for a walk,' she said finally. 'I needed to think. I didn't suppose you'd care. I didn't see what difference it could make.'

Matt's mouth twisted bitterly.

'Did it?' Lesley asked, baffled. 'Make a difference, I mean?'

'Not a bit,' he said sarcastically.

'Well, then . . .'

He scowled, following her into the warmth of the kitchen, practically breathing down her neck, 'Nothing. I just have a sheaf of telephone messages, most of which don't make a bit of sense to me.'

Lesley moved behind one of the chairs, keeping it between the two of them. 'Who called?'

'The receptionist at the dentist first. Uncle Harry asked her to tell you he was going to play checkers at Bert Daley's,' he recited. 'That wasn't too baffling. Then somebody from the Regional Nurses' League. Something about speaking in Boston next month on the fate of abused children?' He looked at her curiously.

Lesley nodded, taking the calendar down and making a note on it. 'Yes, thanks. I told her I'd get back to her.'

'Do you nurse abused children now?'

'I nurse all children now. I have a job with the local school district.' When they had been married and living in New York, she had just been finishing her nursing studies and had taken a job in a dermatologist's office. The hours had been regular and the job uninspiring. But she hadn't minded. Her job had never been her whole life as his had been Matt's. It still wasn't. She found out in Colombia that she empathised more than she sympathised with her patients. When objectivity was called for, she was a dead loss. School nursing was the perfect place for her. She could care deeply about the children and still not be consumed.

'Oh.' Matt took a moment to digest her new occupation. 'Is that all?'

'No.' He shook his head, obviously baffled. 'Just a little while ago two little kids called. Rita, the first one said her name was. Wanted me to tell you she was at Patsy's and would be home at five.' He shrugged, as if he were delivering a message in a foreign tongue. 'Then about ten minutes ago there was a boy.' He groped through his memory. 'Tommy? Terry?'

'Teddy.'

'Yeah, Teddy. Said to tell you he was at Jeremy's and would need a ride.' Matt looked at her, perplexed.

Lesley wasn't. She nodded. 'Was that all?'

'All the phone messages.'

'Thank you.' She turned towards the sheet of cinnamon rolls on the counter, risen now and ready for the oven.

'Lesley,' he put his hand on her arm, stopping her before she reached for them, 'who the hell are Rita and Teddy?'

She drew a deep breath and told him. 'My children.'

CHAPTER THREE

'YOUR . . . *children?*'

Lesley pulled away from him and reached for the baking-sheet, then turned, holding it as a barrier between them. 'That's right.'

It looked for a moment as if her words had knocked the breath right out of him. Then he steadied himself. 'What's going on?' he demanded. 'What children?'

Lesley carried the rolls to the oven and put them in before she turned around to answer him. As she did so, she thrust her chin out in defiance, then wrapped her arms across her chest defensively. 'I adopted them.'

'Adopted them?' Matt looked as if she were speaking Martian. Lesley wasn't surprised. She was sure children were the furthest thing from his mind. They always had been. Even when their marriage had been intact, children had never been on Matt Colter's agenda. She had found that out fast enough.

'Teddy is ten and Rita is seven.'

He still didn't say anything, just stared, though she saw something she didn't quite comprehend flicker in his eyes.

'They're from Colombia,' she went on determinedly.

'Columbia?'

She nodded. At least he was responding.

'South Carolina?'

She shook her head. 'South America. They were orphaned, in the earthquake near San Fabio.'

He grimaced. 'That was a bad one.'

'Yes, it was terrible.' The memories could still make her shudder.

Matt blinked, something in her manner making him ask, 'You were there?'

29

'Yes.'

'Dammit, Lesley!' he burst out. 'What in heaven's name for?'

'I was nursing.'

He looked at her as if she'd said she solicited on street corners. 'You worked for Dr Conlon.'

'I quit.'

'When?' He shoved his hands into the pockets of his jeans and leaned against the counter, scowling at her.

'A few weeks after . . .' She didn't have to say after what. He knew.

'Just "quit"?' He looked baffled.

'Why not?' Lesley countered. 'What did I have to hang around for?'

'You lived there——'

'Correction: we camped there.' They had had a lovely brownstone in the East Eighties. A fashionable address, exactly the sort of one that an up-and-coming foreign correspondent ought to have when he was home, however infrequently that might be. It had belonged to Matt's parents, who had bestowed it on their son and his new wife shortly after their wedding.

Lesley would have loved turning it into a home if she'd had someone to share that home with. As it was, the wedding presents weren't even unpacked before Matt was gone the first time. And they gathered dust while Lesley slept in their big lonely bed by herself and cooked meals for one while Matt roamed the hotspots of the world.

'So you just up and went to Colombia instead?'

'First I came back here. Then I applied to an overseas nursing programme. When I got an assignment, I went.' She made it sound far simpler than it had been. A small-town girl, she had never done the sort of globe-trotting that Matt took for granted. She had been apprehensive but determined. If the outside world had lured her husband away from her, she wanted to know what was so wonderful about it.

'They sent a greenhorn into a disaster area?' He looked appalled, dark brows furrowing over angry eyes.

'They sent a qualified nurse into a rural village to care for expectant mothers and children. I just happened to be there when the earthquake hit.'

'Hell!' Matt swallowed hard, his face pale. He licked his lips and expelled a shaky breath. 'Were you . . . hurt?'

'A few scratches.' Lesley gave him a wintry smile. 'I seem to be just as indestructible as you are.'

He looked back. 'So, what . . . happened?'

'I did more than take care of expectant mothers and babies. And I eventually became a mother myself. Teddy and Rita's mother was one of the women in the village who helped me. She shared her house with me, made me welcome. Her husband had died when Rita was a baby. It was just Manuela, Rita, Teddy—his name was Teo, then—and their old grandmother. Rita and Teddy were at school the morning of the quake. I was at the clinic. Manuela and her mother were . . . at home.' She stopped, swallowed, then forced herself to go on again. 'They were crushed by the rubble.'

Matt closed his eyes.

'Teddy and Rita and I just sort of banded together after that. We didn't have anyone else. I was there for eighteen months, and in that time we became a family. When I came back, there was no question in my mind—they were coming too.' She lifted her chin again, daring him to disagree with what she'd done.

That was something else they had argued about—her devotion to individuals, Matt's to reporting events. No doubt he would have stood amid the rubble, impervious to the suffering, bent only on describing it for the papers back home.

'You can't let yourself get involved,' he'd told her over and over. 'You can't care.'

Well, maybe *he* couldn't. But she had never been able to do otherwise. Caring was what life was all about.

'I understand,' he said simply now, and Lesley, who had been expecting another lecture, was stunned.

'Yes, well . . . I couldn't imagine doing anything else,' she said at last. 'They needed me desperately. And I needed them,' she added truthfully. 'It was hard to say sometimes who was worse off—the dead or the survivors.'

Matt drew an unsteady breath and Lesley looked at him closely.

'I know what you mean.' His voice was ragged. He turned his head away and stared out of the broad kitchen window, down across the garden towards the harbour. A gust of wind sent rain spattering against the window. Far out, the buoy that marked the rocks near Horton's Point clanged with eerie loneliness.

Almost under his breath, Lesley heard Matt repeat, 'I know exactly what you mean.'

What had he survived? she wondered. She wanted to ask him, but the stark look of pain on his face was a strong deterrent. This was a Matt she'd never met before. She knew how to handle him even less well than the Matt she had married. Finally, though, she said, 'I'm sure it was nothing compared to what you suffered.'

He shrugged. 'I managed.' He rummaged in his pocket, extracted a battered pack of cigarettes and a box of matches, and proceeded to light up.

'I thought you'd given it up,' Lesley said. 'I thought you were finally convinced they'd kill you.'

Matt blew out the match and took a long drag. 'Sometimes I think it wouldn't be a bad idea if they did.'

Jolted, she stared at him. 'You don't mean that!'

Matt gave a harsh laugh. 'No, you're right, I probably don't. I wouldn't have gone to such trouble to escape otherwise, would I?' At the moment he looked far from pleased that he had. He stared at the cigarette in his hand, then stubbed it out angrily in the sink. 'So,' he said briskly, 'tell me about the kids.'

Lesley looked at him warily. It was not the sort of

question Matt normally asked. Children didn't interest him. She had suggested they think about starting a family a few months after their wedding, and Matt had looked at her, aghast. 'No way,' he had said. 'No kids.' He hadn't changed his mind by the time he'd left her.

'What do you want to know?'

'How did you get 'em back here, for one thing?'

'On a plane.'

He rolled his eyes. 'I gathered that. I meant, how did you handle the red tape? I know enough to know that international adoptions aren't a piece of cake.'

'No, it wasn't,' Lesley agreed cautiously. She began to run water into the sink to do the washing up from her baking. 'But it was an emergency situation, a hardship. Besides, it wasn't as if they were being dumped on an unsuspecting welfare system. They were going to a family.'

'A family?'

'Well,' Lesley hedged, 'me.'

Matt's brows lifted. 'They let single parents adopt now?'

She didn't answer. Mixing-bowls and utensils clattered noisily in the sink. Her silence was response enough.

'You didn't tell them we were separated,' Matt accused.

She flipped a strand of hair out of her eyes and glowered at him. 'No, I didn't! I didn't see any reason to. I could support them. It wasn't as if I was going to demand anything from you!'

'You just used my name.'

'You were my legal husband!'

'Still am,' he reminded her silkily.

'So, why shouldn't I have? You've enjoyed the convenience of a legal but absent spouse, I'm sure.'

Matt straightened up and moved towards her. 'What the hell's that supposed to mean?'

'It means that I'm sure you found it handy to pull out your marriage to keep any other woman from thinking you might possibly get entangled with her!'

'You're sure, huh?' He practically loomed over her now.

'Did you ever stop to think how many "other women" I've even had occasion to talk to in the last fourteen months, let alone "get entangled" with?'

Lesley backed up a step, coming up hard against the sink. 'Before then,' she insisted. 'And after. You brought up Becca Walsh yourself,' she added recklessly.

Matt said a rude word.

'Don't look so shocked,' he snapped at her when her eyes widened. 'What the hell am I supposed to say when you all but accuse me of adultery? Maybe I ought to be making the same accusation!'

'How dare you?'

'I'll tell you how I dare. I walked back into this house today and overheard you accepting a proposal of marriage. Well, you sure as hell hopped into my bed before we got hitched, sweetheart. What am I supposed to think?'

Lesley's cheeks flamed. Her fists clenched around the soapy sponge, strangling it. 'That was different!'

'Was it?' Matt's look became almost smug. 'I must say, I'm glad to hear it.'

'That's not what I—— Oh, forget it!' Lesley stormed at him. 'Just leave me alone. Get out of here!'

'No, I won't. I can't. I told you—I'm staying right here.'

'Forever?' Lesley mocked him with his earlier declaration.

'Yes.'

She turned her head to look at him. He was leaning against the refrigerator, his expression stubborn as he looked back at her.

'You forget,' she reminded him, hands on her hips, 'we have kids now. At least, I do. And if you stay, they're yours too.'

He nodded his head, confounding her. 'I'm counting on it,' he said, smiling, and turned and walked out of the room.

'So, what's new?' Uncle Harry wandered into the kitchen just before five, beaming as always, asking as always, 'Win the lottery today?'

It was a standing joke between them, a tiny jab at the basically humdrum quality of their existence. Lesley wondered what Harry would say if she told him that winning the lottery would have been a mild shock compared to being proposed to and having Matt walk in in the middle of it.

'Not quite.' She gave him a wan smile.

He hung up his coat, then came over, scrutinising her closely. 'What's the trouble, lovey? You look peaked.'

'He's back,' Lesley said without preamble.

Harry blinked. 'Mm?'

'Matt. He's back.'

'Back where? Here?'

Lesley jerked her head towards the front room. 'In there.'

'Well, I'll be damned!' Harry's eyebrows arched like umbrellas and a smile broke out on his face. 'How is he?'

Rude, Lesley wanted to say. Arrogant. Nasty. Obnoxious. Overbearing. 'The same,' she said.

'None the worse for wear?' Harry seemed unable to stop smiling, even though Lesley was scowling at him.

'Well, I wouldn't say that. He looks . . . ragged. He's still recovering from his wound. He was asleep on the couch a few minutes ago.' After his blunt statement, accepting the children, which she still found hard to credit, he had gone back into the front room, and when she had peeped in she'd found him stretched out on the couch.

'So I should think,' said Harry. 'Well, I'll just see if he's awake yet. I must go talk to the old son of a gun.' He headed for the door to the living-room; then, as if caught by a sudden recollection, he stopped and turned back, looking at his great-niece with concern. 'I didn't think,' he apologised. 'I guess I forgot how things were between you. I mean—how are you?'

'Surviving,' said Lesley, and hoped it was the truth.

She didn't wait around to hear the results of Harry's conversation with Matt. She called Patsy's and said that she would be by to pick Rita up on her way to get Teddy. She didn't want Rita barging in while she was gone. She needed to talk to both the children.

Her discussions with them regarding Matt had been minimal until now. They knew, of course, that she was married to him, but that they were separated. They also knew he'd been a hostage, and they had been as excited as anyone when he'd escaped.

Teddy was thrilled to have a hero for a father, even one he'd never seen. 'I'm so proud of him,' he'd told Lesley with shining eyes the day after Matt's escape had made the headlines. 'I wonder if some day he will be proud of me. Will he like me, do you think?'

'He would like you if he knew you,' Lesley had said. 'But he probably won't ever know you, Teddy. I told you that. We're separated. Now that he's free, I expect we'll divorce.'

'You don't got to,' Teddy had told her, his English awkward, but his sentiment clear enough. 'You could stay married.'

'I don't think so,' Lesley had said, and had changed the subject, not wanting to create false hopes.

For the time being Teddy had let it drop. And when two weeks had passed without his unknown hero-father coming back to claim his mother, nothing more had been said.

Matt's arrival would alter that. But she still didn't want any false hopes, even if he seemed bent on creating them himself.

'I have something to tell you,' she said when she had got both children in the car. They were parked outside Patsy's house, rain still sluicing down, cocooning them in a fogged-window world. Lesley turned and looked at the two of them sitting saucer-eyed in the back seat, and knew they were wondering why she hadn't started the car again and headed for home. 'We have a . . . guest.'

'Who?' Teddy wanted to know.

'Santa Claus?' asked Rita. Her first American Christmas had so enchanted her that Santa had become her favourite person.

'No.' Lesley's fingers twisted on the steering-wheel. 'It's my . . . It's Matt.'

'Matt? Matt Colter? Your husband?' Teddy stared at her, his dark eyes as big as clams.

She nodded.

'Our *papá*?' Rita wanted to know.

'Well, not . . . Yes, I guess so. Sort of,' Lesley hedged.

Teddy was beaming. '*Lo sabía!* I knew it! I knew he'd come.' He bounced up and down on the back seat. 'He's going to stay, no?'

'I . . . don't know.'

'He is,' Teddy said confidently.

'I don't know,' Lesley said even more firmly. 'And you aren't to try to influence him.'

'What's "influence"?' Teddy asked, frowning. His English, which had been marginal when she had brought them here eleven months ago, had improved dramatically. But he still required some explanations, especially when he didn't want to understand.'

'It means you don't tell him you want him to.'

'Why not?' Teddy looked puzzled.

Lesley sucked in her cheeks. 'Just don't, OK?'

Both children looked at her dubiously.

'Don't,' Lesley repeated, and looked at them sternly.

'I don't see——'

'You don't have to see. Just *don't.*'

Mother and son stared at each other for a long moment, then Teddy sighed. 'What's for dinner?'

But, if he was smart enough to change the subject for the moment, he was still out of the car like a shot when Lesley pulled into the garage.

'Hang on!' she called after him. 'We'll all go in together.' She wasn't sure why she thought that was necessary. Several explanations occurred to her. 'Safety in numbers' was the first, though whether it was their safety or her own she had in mind she didn't know.

Matt and Harry were in the living-room, still talking, when she came in, followed by the kids. Teddy was right up there next to her, but Rita hung back, suddenly shy. Both men looked up when they came in, and Matt slowly stood.

'These are . . . my children,' Lesley said hoarsely. 'Teddy.' She put a hand on the boy's shoulder, and then took Rita's hand, drawing the little girl forward. 'And Rita.' Then she turned to them. 'This is . . .' She couldn't say 'your father'. Not if her life had depended on it. 'This is Matt.'

Teddy stuck out his hand eagerly. For a moment Matt just stood there, and Lesley thought, no, he can't be going to ignore Teddy! For all that he might not be fond of kids, she really didn't expect him to do that. But then he did something she expected even less. He ignored Teddy's hand, only to haul the boy into his arms and give him a bear-hug.

Teddy, in Matt's embrace, turned his head slightly to look at Lesley, his eyes widening, questioning; at the same time his mouth was beaming. Then, releasing him, Matt hunkered down and gave Rita an equally warm hug. Lesley stared.

When he stood up again, he had an expression on his face she didn't think she had ever seen before. It was such a blend of tenderness and pain that it tore at her heart.

'I'm glad you're home,' Teddy told him a little stiffly.

Matt smiled. 'I'm glad I'm home too.'

'You're staying?' Rita asked, ignoring Lesley's earlier strictures.

'You'd better believe it,' Matt said.

'Great!' Teddy shot Lesley a triumphant grin, then went right to the heart of things. 'So . . . tell us what happened. How did you really get away?'

Lesley hovered in the doorway, wanting to hear that, but Matt seemed disinclined to satisfy her curiosity. 'Why don't you tell me what you've been doing here?'

Teddy looked briefly disappointed, but, at Matt's

prompting, launched into a tale of his best friend Robby's new rocket. Relieved, Lesley made her escape. But though she fled to the kitchen her mind lingered in the living-room.

Matt's behaviour still astonished her. She had expected a perfunctory acknowledgement of Teddy and Rita. She had imagined a bit of polite small talk, because Matt had social graces even if he didn't have emotional involvement. But she'd never expected bear-hugs.

The memory made her throat tighten and her heart ache. What did it mean? Was he serious about coming back for good? Ashes of nearly dead hopes stirred in her mind, in her heart. Ruthlessly, she squashed them, afraid of them. She'd had them before, plenty of times. Her mother had had them too, about her father.

'You said only hours ago that you'd marry Jacques,' she reminded herself as she prepared supper. 'Are you changing your mind?'

It wasn't a question her mind could grapple with.

When she went to tell Teddy it was time to set the table, she found him perched on the hassock next to the couch where Matt sat. His eyes were glued to the man who was his father, his undivided attention on every word Matt said.

'Time to set the table,' Lesley told him.

Teddy groaned. 'Ah, Mama! Please . . . he was just getting to the good part.'

Lesley gave him an expectant look. Teddy frowned.

'Go on,' Matt said. 'We'll talk later.'

Reluctantly Teddy followed Lesley back into the kitchen.

'What's he telling you?' she demanded.

Teddy's eyes shone. ''Bout when he was in Africa. There was this coup, y'know.'

'I know,' Lesley said sharply, remembering. She'd thought he had died in it. He had been supposed to be sending home stories daily and he had vanished for over a week. It turned out that he'd followed a guerrilla troop into the hills to interview an elusive commander. Getting the interview had been a coup. But his complete disappearance had terrified Lesley.

'He's really brave,' Teddy told her as he set out the plates and silverware. 'I knew he would be.'

Lesley pursed her lips together and thumped the bottle of salad-dressing on the table. Teddy's hero-worship was going to be every bit as bad as she had feared it would be.

The meal, when they finally sat down to it, had an unreal quality. It was so dull, so ordinary, that Lesley had to keep pinching herself to believe that it was really happening—that after all this time Matt was sitting across from her, helping himself to the mashed potatoes and baked chicken, and later to a second slice of pie, while Uncle Harry chuntered on about the weekly paper he edited and Teddy talked about baseball and Rita about the treehouse Patsy's father was going to help the girls build.

Lesley herself didn't say a word. It was beyond her. She could scarcely eat. She stared at her plate and let the conversation wash over her, and every time she looked up she found Matt's eyes on her and she looked quickly away again.

She remembered other meals they had shared around this table when they had first met, meals which they had hardly noticed because they had only had eyes for each other. And when he looked at her the way he was looking at her tonight, all she could think of was where those other meals had led, and the memories made her cheeks burn.

Fortunately, between Teddy and Uncle Harry the conversation rolled along. After the meal, Rita reluctantly loaded the dishwasher while Teddy followed Matt and Uncle Harry back into the living-room to listen as they swapped tales. Lesley took her time rinsing the dishes, and Rita hopped from one foot to the other, exhorting her mother to hurry.

'What's the rush?' Lesley wanted to know.

Rita shot her an exasperated look. 'I'm missing everything!' She shoved the last of the plates into the dishwasher and said, 'There! Am I done now?'

'Yes, you're done.' But Rita was through the door before she got the words out of her mouth.

Lesley couldn't decide whether to follow her or not. She felt almost like a prisoner in her own kitchen. But when she went into the living-room she would have to face Matt, and she simply couldn't.

There had been too much said between them already today. Too many emotions had already flared to life. She heard the sound of both men's voices, Rita's giggle, Teddy's chirping questions, and knew she couldn't face it. She made herself a cup of tea, fetched a book, and sat at the table pretending to read until it was time for the children to go to bed.

They went, but reluctantly, and only when they had been assured by Matt and, grudgingly, by Lesley, that he would indeed be there when they got up in the morning.

'You ought to turn in too,' Harry was telling him when Lesley came back downstairs from tucking in the children. 'You look beat.'

'I'm . . . tired,' Matt admitted. He looked at Lesley, his expression expectant.

She said grudgingly, 'There's a spare bed in Teddy's room already made up.'

Uncle Harry made a disapproving noise which only made her spine stiffer.

Matt gave her a sardonic smile. 'Like that, is it?'

Lesley nodded. 'I'll put out a fresh towel and washcloth for you.'

'Just like company.'

'Yes.'

'Thanks.' His tone was sarcastic.

She ignored it. 'I'm going up now too.'

Uncle Harry shook his head in disapproval. 'I'd imagine you and Matt would have a lot to talk about.'

He imagined right. But she didn't think she was capable of it tonight. She was too confused by her feelings, by his declarations and actions. Yes, of course, they would have to talk. But not now. Not tonight.

'I'm sure Matt's tired,' Lesley countered. 'And I know I am. There'll be plenty of time to chat.'

'Chat?' Uncle Harry echoed, disbelieving. But Lesley didn't reply. She fled up the stairs as if all the devils in hell were after her.

It was twenty-past three when Lesley awoke from a fitful, dream-filled sleep. For a moment she didn't remember why she should feel so apprehensive. Then it all came back to her in one word—Matt.

She rolled over and punched her pillow, telling herself not to think about him. But she was awake now and couldn't help it. Besides, she saw a line of light under the door. Harry must have left the light on downstairs. Either that or he hadn't gone to bed yet.

Sometimes he didn't. Nights were the hardest time for him, the time when he missed Leila the most. On several occasions since Leila's death, Lesley had got up to find him sitting downstairs, sometimes in the light, sometimes in the dark, rocking slowly back and forth in the cane rocker.

The first time she had asked him, worried, if he was all right.

He had smiled at her, a pain-filled smile, bitter-sweet and aching. 'As good as I'll ever be, sweetheart. I'm just thinking . . . remembering Leila.'

'I remember her too,' Lesley had said. And she had made them cups of cocoa, and they had drunk them, reminiscing together, until finally Harry had stood up and stretched, then reached out and tousled her hair.

'Thank you,' he'd said simply. 'I reckon I'll nod off now.'

He had, quickly and easily. The next time she had found him up, they had done it again.

They would do it again tonight, Lesley decided as she got out of bed and pulled on her lightweight robe. She wouldn't mind a bit of reminiscence about Leila right now. It would be far better, now she was awake, to do that than to lie up here tossing and turning and thinking about Matt.

But Harry wasn't in his rocking-chair. She called his name softly and got no response. He must have simply forgotten to turn off the light. She was just about to flick it off and go back up when she heard a sound out on the glassed-in porch. Curious, she went to investigate.

'Harry?' She stuck her head around the corner, peering into the darkness.

For a moment there was silence. Then the day-bed creaked and she heard, 'No. It's me.'

Matt.

Lesley's mouth went dry. She hovered, suspended, uncertain. But at last concern won out over cowardice, and, pulling her robe more closely around her to ward off the springtime coolness, she ventured into the room. 'Are you . . . all right?'

'Yeah.'

She saw the orange glow at the tip of the cigarette that he brought to his lips. He wasn't looking towards her, but instead kept his gaze fixed on the lighthouse on the point. Even his profile looked tired.

'I haven't been sleeping much,' he said after a moment. 'It's no big deal.'

'It's called "post-traumatic stress syndrome",' Lesley told him.

He took a long drag on the cigarette. 'Putting a name on it doesn't seem to make it go away, though.'

Lesley knew that. 'You keep remembering?' she ventured.

'You don't forget,' he said harshly. The pain was heavy in his words.

'Did they . . .? What did they . . .?' But she couldn't ask the question.

'Do to me?' His voice was bitter. 'Well, they didn't torture me—not exactly. They didn't do any of the stuff you read about, at least. But it is torture, really, expecting to die every day. And after a while——' he raked a hand through his hair '—hell, I don't know. Maybe I torture myself.'

'Why?' Lesley asked. 'What happened?'

But he simply shook his head, shutting her out. 'It's over,' he said gruffly. 'Forget it.'

'But . . .'

'I said, forget it!' His tone was curt. It was a tone she recognised, a tone she'd come to hate. It meant that the walls were coming down between them, that he was shutting her out once more.

Lesley cleared her throat, determined to leave before she was dismissed. 'Consider it forgotten,' she said remotely. 'I just saw the light and thought Uncle Harry might have forgotten to turn it off. Obviously I was wrong. Goodnight.' She swung around and started back towards the living-room when his voice stopped her.

'Les . . .'

She paused, turning back slowly, confused by the sudden urgency she heard in his voice.

'Don't!'

She stopped, but her feelings of trepidation didn't. 'Don't what?'

'Go.'

She didn't. She waited, hovering indecisively.

He cleared his throat. 'I mean, Harry was right. We . . . we really haven't talked.'

'We've argued.'

'Yes, but . . .' He shook his head wearily. 'I didn't want to.'

'You sounded as if you did.'

He scowled and straightened up slightly. 'Well, how the hell would you feel in the same situation? That jerk Dubois had just proposed to you!'

'He's not a jerk.'

'Matter of opinion. Anyway, it wasn't exactly the scenario my dreams had been made of.'

Lesley looked at him curiously. 'You dreamed?'

'Of course I did.' He stubbed out the cigarette irritably.

'What else was I supposed to do?'

'I . . . don't know.' She had dreamed herself, fantasised. But she couldn't imagine Matt having done that. He was too pragmatic, too disciplined.

'Well, I did,' he said gruffly. 'And it sure as hell wasn't to come home to my wife accepting another man's proposal.'

'What did you dream?'

He looked away. 'A lot of foolishness, it appears.'

'What?' she insisted.

He shifted his gaze and glared at her now, goaded. 'That I'd come home and find you waiting to throw your arms around me! That you'd want to start over again, do things right this time! Asinine, wasn't it?'

Lesley just stared, astonished.

Matt snorted. 'Well, that pretty much answers my question. I thought you said you needed sleep?' he demanded irritably. 'Then why don't you go to bed?'

'You asked me to stay,' she reminded him, her mind still spinning from his revelation.

'My mistake,' he said roughly. 'Don't let me keep you. Goodnight.'

But Lesley didn't move. Had he really dreamt that? Did he really want to start over again? Once more hope quickened inside her.

'What are you waiting for? Go,' Matt bit out.

'But, Matt——'

'Forget it!' He lurched to his feet and jerked open the front door. 'I shouldn't have said anything.' And before she could speak again he had limped off into the night.

A part of her wanted to run after him. Common sense and cold feet kept her rooted to the spot. But, as she watched him disappear down the road, she was assailed by so many differing emotions that she couldn't sort them out.

The Matt who had stalked back into her life today was far more confusing than the man who had left her. Granted, that man had been just as dogmatic, just as arrogant, but he had never shown half the emotions she had seen in this one.

Was it merely a reaction to his captivity? Was he simply trying to get his feet on the ground again before he resumed his regular life-style? Did he figure he could get readjusted more quickly if he hung around her?

It didn't seem unlikely.

She went back up to her bed. But she lay there, eyes open, and hugged the pillow against her chest. For months she had dreamed of Matt coming home to her, of his saying the very words he had said this afternoon. 'I'm staying. For ever.'

And now that he'd said them, it was worse.

Oh, Lesley, don't wish for it, she warned herself. He's hurt you before. He'll hurt you again. Leopards don't change their spots. She had only to remember her own father to verify that.

She had made a life for herself without Matt once. She didn't want to become like her mother, destined to repeat the same mistake over and over again.

Still, all the warnings in the world seemed to do her little good where Matt Colter was concerned. She only had to see him again to feel exactly the same longing she had felt the first time she even knew he was alive.

The first time she had seen him, he'd been asleep exactly where she'd left him tonight. She had been spending the summer before her last year at nursing school with her great-aunt and uncle, and she had just gone for a long walk on the rocks, trying to convince herself that a deeper relationship with Jacques Dubois was what she wanted, and, distracted, she had come up the front steps of the house, opened the door to the porch, and had found the man of her dreams asleep on the bed.

She had stopped, stunned. All the rational arguments for getting serious with Jacques that she had come up with evaporated in a moment. In the face of vague girlish fantasies, they had seemed worthy indeed. In the face of the most gorgeously attractive man she'd ever seen, they were like so much thin air.

She had, of course, told herself that simply seeing a gorgeous, rugged male shouldn't make a difference. Especially a sound-asleep one. Heaven only knew, when he opened his eyes and mouth, the illusion of perfection would doubtless be shattered.

But then he did. And his eyes were a deep, dark brown, warm with sleep, and glinting, first with interest and then amusement, as he saw her gaping at him, her mouth opening and closing like a fish.

He spoke, and his deep voice sent a shiver right down her spine. Even now she could remember thinking how unfair it was that a man with everything else going for him should have such a wonderful voice as well.

'Am I sleeping in your bed, sweetheart?' he asked her in a sleep-roughened baritone that melted her where she stood.

'I wish you were,' she blurted out, unthinking, and immediately turned scarlet when his laugh boomed out.

He sat up, stretched, giving her a view of several inches of muscular abdomen as his shirt lifted away from the waistband of his trousers. Then he unfolded himself and stood up, offering her his hand. 'Before we head in that direction, perhaps we should at least introduce ourselves,' he said, still smiling. 'I'm Matt Colter.'

Lesley swallowed, still blushing furiously. 'I—didn't mean that. I mean, I meant it, but I shouldn't have said it. I mean——Oh, heavens, I think I'd better give an assumed name.'

It wouldn't have helped if she had, for at that moment Leila appeared in the doorway between the porch and the living-room and said, 'Ah, Matt, I see you've met Lesley. She's the niece I've been telling you about.'

'And even better in person,' Matt said, still holding Lesley's hand. He glanced down at her, grinning broadly. Then he winked a conspirator's wink, and Lesley gulped, mortified, though something in her wanted nothing more than to laugh too.

'She's going to give me a tour of the house,' Matt told

Leila. 'Starting with her bedroom,' he added slyly, still grinning.

Leila made a tsking sound. 'Just as long as you don't end there. Go on, then, the two of you.' She shooed them towards the stairs. 'Afterwards, take him down to the harbour, Lesley. He hasn't been there. Be back by six. Harry will be home and we'll be having dinner.'

Lesley tried to think up some excuse, some reason why she couldn't possibly spend the rest of the afternoon in the company of this handsome, laughing man. But she couldn't. And, if the truth were known, she didn't want to. Even though he'd embarrassed her—even though she'd embarrassed herself—she didn't want to walk away from him.

'Follow me,' she said.

He did. For the rest of the day.

And whatever spark had flared up between them grew.

Lesley showed him the house—including her bedroom, which he pronounced delightful, even going so far as to bounce on the bed and wink at her while she, scandalised, couldn't help but laugh.

Then he took her hand and said, 'Show me more,' and she did, taking him round the entire village, showing him the general store, the newspaper office where Uncle Harry was, the school she had attended, the white-steepled church. Then they walked down by the harbour where, fortunately, because it was midday, she did not run into Jacques Dubois, and finally along the beach where she had walked not so many hours before the earth had shifted on its axis.

Perhaps it was youthful exaggeration, but it seemed to Lesley as if the whole universe had changed in the span of mere moments. Matt made the sun shine more brightly, made the sea sparkle more vividly. He made the birds' calls louder, the trees greener. He brought three dimensions to Lesley's two-dimensional life. She had never met a man like him. The more she knew of Matthew Colter, the more she wanted to know.

And her feelings it seemed, were shared by Matt.

They spent nearly every moment together, packing more living into the next few days than Lesley had packed into the last few years.

If she had been indecisive and tentative about her relationship with Jacques Dubois, she wasn't that way about Matt. And there was nothing tentative at all about Matthew Colter. When he wanted something, he went after it.

And he wanted Lesley. A lot.

She had read the phrase, 'He eats little girls like you,' countless times. But she'd never met a man it applied to until she met Matt. He didn't eat her, but he looked as if he wished he could.

His eyes followed her hungrily wherever she moved. If she had an errand to run, he ran it with her. If she had a chore to do for Aunt Leila, he volunteered to help. Where Lesley was, Matt was, every waking moment. And if they were apart to sleep—well, that wasn't Matt's idea.

'I thought you came to see me,' Uncle Harry complained when he hadn't had more than a glimpse of Matt in twenty-four hours.

'That was before I found out there was better scenery in the neighbourhood,' Matt countered apologetically as he snaked his arm around Lesley's waist and hauled her hard against him. 'Much better.'

'Mind your manners, Matthew Colter,' Aunt Leila admonished him, but there was a tolerant twinkle in her eye as she spoke.

She admonished Lesley too, later on.

'You be careful now,' she told her great-niece. 'He's not the settling-down sort.'

But Lesley didn't have to be warned, she could see that for herself. It just didn't matter. She had never felt like this before. And nothing—not even common sense, not even her mother's experience—was going to come between her and the most fascinating man she had ever met.

To Leila's everlasting astonishment, Matt seemed equally smitten. He might have come for the weekend, but he stayed a week. And when he left, having received an urgent summons to Paris to cover a political scandal, he promised to be back as soon as he could.

'A week, no more,' he assured Lesley.

Privately Leila told her to expect him when she saw him. 'That's the way it is,' she said. 'You never know.'

To Leila's amazement, however, Matt was back in five days. And, to her further amazement, he stayed another week and a half. At the end of that time, instead of walking Lesley out to the end of the point and bidding her a fond farewell, he walked her out to the end of the point and asked her to marry him.

She said yes.

The idyll had ended there. Marriage had been anything but happy ever after. It had been the greatest agony she had ever suffered in her life. She had survived it once, barely. She knew she wouldn't make it again. She had loved him too much the first time.

Yes, she would care. She couldn't help but care. She couldn't help but love. She had, if the truth were known, never stopped loving Matthew, even as she had more or less accepted the proposal from Jacques. It was just that she understood about different forms of love now. The love she felt for Matt, through its very intensity, could not help but burn her. So she would continue to love him, but only from a distance. That was the only way she could save herself from hurt. She might want to believe in dreams. But reality, she knew, was what life was all about.

And the reality was that she did not dare to let him rend her heart in two again.

CHAPTER FOUR

IT might have been cowardly, but Lesley had never claimed to be brave. It might have been running away, but Lesley had never seen much virtue in standing her ground in a losing fight. In the morning Lesley took Rita to Freeport to go shopping.

'You need summer clothes,' she told her daughter. 'We'll make a day of it.'

'A whole day?' Rita's eyes shone.

'Well, I said I would,' Lesley defended her sudden decision, 'when the weather warmed up.'

'Yeah, but I didn't think today.' Rita looked dubiously out of the window at the mud-brown landscape and the trees still virtually leafless.

'What's wrong with today?' Lesley asked somewhat sharply.

'Well, you know . . . there's Matt, and . . .' Rita was watching her mother thoughtfully, seeing far more, Lesley feared, than she wanted the child to see.

'Matt will need rest.'

'Yes, but——'

'Patsy can come too,' offered Lesley, raising the enticement.

Rita brightened. 'And for the whole day?'

'Yes.' Lesley tipped cereal into a bowl for Rita and glanced at the clock. 'But you'd better call right now because I want to leave early.'

'It doesn't take long, does it?'

'About two hours,' Lesley said, handing Rita the milk carton.

Uncle Harry came in, his bedroom slippers shuffling across the floor. 'Where you off to?' he asked his niece.

'Freeport.'

'Freeport?' He raised his eyebrows.

Lesley took a deep breath. 'Why not?'

'Matt . . .'

'Matt has nothing to do with this. Rita has outgrown nearly all her clothes. The weather is turning warm, and we need to get some more.'

'Gordons' don't suit you?'

Gordons' was the local all-in-one store that carried everything from envelopes to cough drops to Buster Brown shirts and shoes. It suited up to a point. But it didn't suit Lesley today. 'There's better selection in Freeport,' she said, pouring him his wake-up cup of coffee. 'And the sooner we get going, the more chance we'll have to look around.' And the less chance she would have of being here to run into Matt when he got up.

With luck she would be well on her way before he set foot out of the bedroom. She'd heard him come upstairs finally about four-thirty. She'd heard his footsteps pause momentarily outside her door. She'd remembered a time when he had opened that door and come to her. She'd held her breath. He'd gone on by.

But the memories kept her awake the rest of the night. They were too real—he was too real—for her to pretend indifference, no matter how much she would have liked to.

So flight seemed the best alternative, at least for the moment. There was always the chance, she told herself, that with his short attention span, by the time she got home this afternoon he would already be gone.

Harry snorted at her reasons for going, but Lesley was impervious. 'Can I bring you anything?' she asked him.

'Not a thing,' he told her, then eyed her over the top of his mug. 'But you might buy yourself a quart of gumption while you're there.'

Lesley felt the flush climb up her cheeks even as she resolutely ignored him and helped herself to a bowl of cereal. 'Call Patsy,' she told her daughter. 'We want an early start.'

Rita finished her cereal, then went to call her friend, coming back moments later to announce, 'Patsy can go. I told her to hurry. She'll be ready in half an hour.'

'Fine. We'll do these dishes and then I'll get the car out of the garage,' Lesley said.

'Bit of a rush, isn't it?' Uncle Harry pushed his glasses up further on his nose and regarded her closely.

Lesley rinsed out her own coffee-cup, deliberately keeping her back to him. 'Not really.'

'So what'll I tell Matt?'

Rita, who was half-way out of the door to sit on the steps and wait for Patsy, halted in her tracks at this intriguing question.

'Whatever you like,' Lesley said shortly. 'I doubt it will matter to him. Go on, Rita, or I'll have you helping with the dishes.'

Rita went, but not without a backward glance at her mother.

'Have you talked to him at all?' Harry asked her.

'Some. Last night,' Lesley admitted. 'I woke up and thought you'd left the light on. He was down there.'

'And?'

Lesley shrugged. 'And nothing. We just talked.'

'What do you think?'

She gave another shrug.

Uncle Harry made a tsking sound and shook his head. 'Not like you, Lesley. Not like you at all.'

She turned on him, glaring. 'What am I supposed to think? What am I supposed to say? He says he's staying, but he's made promises before. Just the way my father promised my mother. Well, I'm not going to be my mother. I've been through it once with him, and I won't do it again! It hurt too much the first time.'

'Things change,' Harry said mildly, taking a sip of coffee.

'Things, maybe. But not Matt Colter. He's carved in stone.'

'Was,' Harry corrected.

'And he's not now?' Lesley didn't believe that.

'I think there are a few cracks.'

'Why? What did he say?' She couldn't suppress her interest, in spite of her better judgement.

Harry shrugged. 'Didn't say much. It's just an—impression.'

Lesley made a face. She had once had the impression that they shared a love that would endure forever. She'd never been more wrong. She wiped the kitchen table, then topped up Uncle Harry's coffee-cup. 'There's a soup pot heating on the back of the stove. You can have it for lunch if you want. Or sandwiches. Teddy went out early with Robby Ferris. They're fishing off the point with Robby's dad.'

She had been delighted when Robby had called at daybreak with the invitation. And equally delighted that Teddy had only cast a longing backward glance at the sleeping man in the other bed before slipping into his clothes, eating a hurried breakfast, and dashing out to join his friend.

'He should stay out of your hair most of the day. But if he comes back early, you might try to keep him out of Matt's. He's bursting with questions.'

'Some of us are,' Harry commented drily.

Lesley pursed her lips. 'Yes, well, I doubt Matt will be bursting to answer. And he's not keen on children.' Especially his own, she might have added.

'Don't fret,' Harry told her. 'It might be good for him. And it won't hurt Teddy.'

'I don't know about that.'

Uncle Harry frowned. 'What do you mean?'

'What if he thinks Matt will stay?'

'What if Matt does stay?' Harry asked her calmly.

But Lesley wouldn't let herself consider that. She turned away and banged the cereal bowls in the sink.

'Everything will work out,' Uncle Harry promised.

'Please God,' Lesley muttered. But she wasn't sure.

The trip down to Freeport gave her plenty of time to think as the girls entertained each other. But once they had arrived, she had to devote all her energy to supervising them. Shopping with two seven-year-olds was an exhausting proposition. They chattered to each other and to her, asking questions, making comments, hauling her from one shop to another along Freeport's busy streets. It was big-city-living for both girls, and they were enthralled.

It was a great antidote, Lesley found. Or, if not an antidote, at least an effective postponement for dealing with what ailed her. She was exhausted when at last the girls wanted to stop for one last look at the toys in a shop.

Lesley, who had had her fill of shopping of all kinds by that time, declined. 'You go ahead,' she said, stopping at the entry. 'I'll just stand here and wait.'

It wouldn't be too boring, she thought, as there was a television and stereo-equipment store next to it, and she had her choice of twenty different sets, each playing a different channel in demonstration. 'I'll meet you here in ten minutes.'

'OK.' And the girls trooped off.

On one screen the Red Sox were playing out West where it was sunny and about twenty degrees warmer than it was here, and Lesley stared distractedly at the game. Next to it a punk rock group were gyrating around a psychedelic set, while on another screen the Secretary of State was being quizzed by a television news commentator. She scanned them all, not really captured by any until one familiar face caught her eye.

It was Hank Griswald, one of the foreign service officials who had escaped with Matt, meeting the Press on Sunday afternoon television.

'. . . harrowing,' he was saying, in response to one of the questions. 'Risky, of course. But Colter was thorough—meticulous, in fact. And positive it would work.' A satisfied smile creased his weathered face. 'And he was right. He was definitely the hero of the piece.'

'It came off without a hitch, all right,' the commentator

went on. 'Other than Colter's leg wound and one terrorist gunned down accidentally by his own compatriots, your escape was relatively bloodless.'

'Yes.'

'How did Colter manage it?'

Lesley leaned towards the screen intently.

'I'm not entirely sure.' Griswald stretched his long frame, making himself more comfortable in the armchair in which he sat. 'He'd been there longer than most of us, got to know things, people. Made contacts, perhaps. I don't know what he did, really. But he passed the word a week or so before we made the escape. Asked if we were game. Of course we were.'

'But you don't know how he arranged it?'

Griswald shook his head.

'He never said?'

'Not a word.'

'And he hasn't said much since, has he?' the commentator persisted. 'There've been a lot of articles, but no interviews, though lots of people have been trying to get his story.'

Griswald permitted himself a dry smile. 'Perhaps he intends to write it himself. It's what he does, you know.'

'Perhaps,' the commentator assented, then went on conversationally, 'You know he's disappeared?'

Griswald straightened in his chair.

Lesley, who had been leaning against the wall, jerked upright, her eyes widening as she stared at the screen.

'That's right.' A brief glimpse of the commentator showed him with a smug smile at Griswald's astonishment. 'Ex-hostage hero Matt Colter has dropped out of sight. Walked out of his colleague Becca Walsh's house on Friday night and hasn't been seen since. What do you think happened to him?'

Griswald shook his head. 'I've no idea,' he said. 'Perhaps he's gone off to write.'

'You don't suspect foul play?' the commentator probed. 'Another kidnapping?'

Griswald laughed. 'Not a bit. He may be licking his wounds, figuratively speaking. Taking a break—goodness knows, he could use one. One would have to after he'd been through that. I'm sure he's not himself yet. But you'll see him again before too long. In Poland or Morocco or India. Wherever there's a story,' Hank Griswald promised, 'Matt Colter will be there.'

The words echoed in Lesley's head long after the station had taken a commercial break, and they still spun in her mind during the long drive home. Griswald was undoubtedly right, she thought as she absent-mindedly shepherded the girls out to the car for the return trip to Day's Harbor—Matt wasn't himself yet.

He had just been through a harrowing experience, one he certainly couldn't have recovered from completely. Right now he probably really didn't know what he wanted. But, when he was feeling up to par and a story broke anywhere on the globe, it wouldn't matter what he had told her about staying, Colter would be there.

But he was still in Day's Harbor when Lesley got back.

In fact, when she pulled up to the house, she could see him lying in a hammock in the front garden, watching Teddy throw a frisbee for the dog to chase. He lifted his head when she got out of the car, but otherwise he made no response. For her part, Lesley determined not to either. She gathered her parcels together and disappeared into the house.

Harry was sitting on the porch doing the crossword. Lesley dumped her bags on the day-bed, then flung herself down into the rocking-chair.

'I see he's still here.' She knew she sounded like a petulant child, but she couldn't help it.

'Yes,' a voice behind her drawled before Uncle Harry could speak, and she spun around to see Matt slowly mounting the steps. 'He told you he would be. So you might as well get used to it.'

'You——'

'I've been invited to,' he drawled, cutting her off.

Lesley glared at Harry accusingly. He gave an eloquent 'not me' shrug.

'Not Harry,' Matt said. 'Teddy. *Our* son.'

Lesley's eyes narrowed. '*My* son.'

Matt nodded. 'And mine. You told me so.'

'I also told you that you had no real responsibility for him. You were purely a name on an official paper. It could have been anyone.'

'No, it couldn't,' Matt contradicted her silkily. 'It could only have been your husband.'

'You're not my husband any more.'

'In name I am.'

And, heaven help her, in her heart. But such thoughts paved the way to future heartbreak, so she drew in a long breath and said carefully, 'But that's all.'

Matt met her eyes for a moment. His were dark and unfathomable, his face mostly pale, though there was a flush along his cheekbones and his eyes seemed to glitter almost feverishly. 'Then it's where we'll have to start.'

They stared at each other, neither willing to give an inch. Finally Lesley said, 'You're a missing person, do you know that?'

Uncle Harry's eyebrows snapped up.

Matt shrugged, but looked irritated.

'Says who?' Uncle Harry asked.

'Network news. I first heard it this afternoon as part of an interview with Griswald.'

Matt's eyes narrowed. 'What did he say?'

'That you were a hero.'

'I'm not a hero!'

His vehemence startled her so much that she took a step backwards. 'He meant you were the one who arranged——'

'I know I arranged it,' Matt said bitterly.

'Then——'

'It doesn't make me a hero.'

He'd never eschewed heroics before. She looked at him warily, weighing this new attitude, not coming to any satisfying conclusions.

'Damn Griswald,' he muttered, slamming his hand into his fist. 'Why the hell doesn't he just shut up?'

'He sounded impressed.'

'He shouldn't be. What else did he say?'

'That he didn't expect you'd been kidnapped a second time.'

Matt smiled bitterly. 'Too right.'

'And,' she went on, 'that you'd probably just gone off to lick your wounds, but that you'd be back.'

'He was wrong about that.' Matt's tone was abrupt. Almost at once he turned to Uncle Harry, who had been watching the exchange as if he were sitting at the centre court at Wimbledon. 'I thought the whole thing would have blown over by now. But if he keeps yakking . . . I'd appreciate it if you wouldn't spread the news of my presence around.'

'No fear.' Harry gave him a comradely smile. 'I won't breathe a word.'

Matt looked once more at Lesley. 'And you?'

If she said she would shout his presence from the rooftops, would he leave? She doubted it.

Besides, she told herself, the less attention called to Matt, the less disruption would occur in her own life. When he finally did decide to be on his way, she didn't want to be left here looking jilted again and fielding asinine questions from the Press and half the town.

'My lips are sealed,' she assured him.

'Thank you.' He inclined his head.

Teddy came loping across the yard. 'Hey, Dad—c'mon! Don't you want to see what else Rufe can do?' He and the dog were still cavorting on the lawn.

Dad? Lesley's stomach plummeted. Her gaze flicked to Matt, curious about his reaction. To her surprise, he smiled. 'I'm coming!' he called, and turned to go down the steps.

'He's the one you want to talk to,' Lesley said to his back.

'Huh?' Matt glanced over his shoulder.

'Teddy. He'll be the one to spread the news.'

Matt shook his head. 'He won't. I've asked him.'

Lesley grimaced doubtfully. 'He was certainly eager enough for you to——' She broke off, not wanting to discuss Teddy's earlier reactions.

'Eager for me to what?'

She fixed her gaze on the lighthouse in the distance. 'Nothing.'

Matt turned and came to stand squarely in front of her, looming over her, breathing down the front of her shirt. 'Certainly eager for me to what?'

Lesley sighed and shrugged. 'He . . . wondered when you'd come.'

'Here?'

'Yes.'

'When I got back to the States, you mean? After . . .?'

'Yes.' There was a ship passing on the horizon, but it was too far out for her to make out much detail. She tried, though, ignoring him.

'He *wanted* me to come?'

Lesley still didn't look at him. 'Yes,' she said shortly.

'Then why the hell didn't you bring them to Washington?'

She jerked around and stared at him then, forgetting Harry's presence, forgetting everything except how unfair he was. Bring *them* to Washington? She had doubted he'd even welcome her!

'Oh, sure,' she said sarcastically. 'I was supposed to just run right down and throw my arms around you and then say, "By the way, I'd like you to meet our kids!" Maybe you've forgotten your attitude towards kids. Especially *our* kids!' She glared at him, her eyes spitting fire. Uncle Harry looked more intrigued by the minute.

Matt's eyes flickered away for a moment, and she thought

she had made her point. But then they came back to challenge hers squarely. 'A man can change his mind.'

Lesley weighed that. 'Maybe,' she allowed. 'But I've never seen you do it. Besides, you were fairly clear on the subject once before.'

'Lesley.' Matt gave her a warning look, his eyes skating towards Uncle Harry, who had given up the crossword for the more interesting pursuit of shameless eavesdropping.

She had never mentioned it in front of Harry before, but now, goaded, she couldn't see why she shouldn't. 'He didn't want kids,' she said baldly to her uncle. 'A wife was bad enough.'

'That's not what I said!' Matt exploded.

'Close enough.'

Matt let out his breath in a furious hiss.

'Bring them to Washington,' Lesley mused, still annoyed. 'Maybe I should have. I could have brought them to you at Becca's.' She gave a short, harsh laugh. 'I almost wish I had! I'd have liked to see her face.'

'Forget Becca Walsh.' Matt's voice was sharp.

'How can I?' she retorted. 'She was like the cuckoo in our marriage. Five minutes alone together and pop! There she was.'

'She was just doing her job.'

'No doubt she'll be around to do it again,' Lesley predicted, and before Matt could reply she turned smartly on her heel and went into the house.

She tried to put him out of her mind, but it was impossible. All the time Lesley was preparing supper, she found herself glancing out of the window to where he still lay in the hammock. And her annoyance grew when she discovered that not only Teddy seemed enchanted by their visitor, but that Rita had been captivated as well.

Her daughter had carried the new clothes they had bought up to her bedroom soon after they got home. Less than half an hour later, Lesley heard her clattering back up the stairs and down again, her arms filled with parcels.

'Where are you going with those?'

'Matt wants to see them.'

Lesley snorted her disbelief. But the unlikelihood of Matt Colter being interested in a seven-year-old girl's new T-shirts and shorts was lost on Rita. She gave her mother a baffled look and banged out of the door, then skipped across the yard, singing out, 'Here they are. Just look, Matt—er—Dad. Wait till you see!'

Matt, Lesley noted to her consternation, swung himself to a sitting position, making room for the small dark-haired girl to snuggle up beside him. Easing his stiff leg away from her, he was still able to hug her against him, and together, chatting and laughing, they went through Rita's purchases.

Lesley bit her lip. It was totally unfair how comfortable they looked together, how right. It made her throat tighten and brought a stinging wetness to her eyes. Matt looked as if he belonged with kids, as if he were made to be a father.

Which just went to show, she reminded herself, how little appearances could be trusted.

By the time Lesley had called everyone to supper, she had her scepticism firmly in place, but Teddy and Rita had the shiny eyes and glowing smiles of the newly converted.

'Dad says maybe we can go to a Red Sox game, Mama,' Teddy told her, beaming.

Lesley gave Matthew a narrow-eyed look which he met with an innocence that galled her.

'And he says I can come too,' Rita chimed in.

'You don't know nothing about baseball,' Teddy informed her loftily.

'She can learn,' Matt put in. 'Maybe you can have a sports column,' he suggested to Harry.

'Who would write it?' Harry wanted to know.

'Me.'

'For how long?' scoffed Lesley, but Matt didn't answer.

Harry, however, said, 'I'll consider that. If you're interested in it, I could use a bit of help down t'paper. When you're feeling up to it, of course.'

'Sure,' Matt said easily. 'Sounds great.'

Lesley bit her tongue. Matt Colter working on a two-bit Maine weekly? Sure.

But Matt just gave her a blithe smile. Lesley didn't smile back.

The phone rang and Teddy leaped to get it. 'It's probably Robby,' he said. 'He said he'd call. He's shootin' off his rocket tonight.'

But it wasn't Robby. A moment later Teddy held out the receiver towards his mother. 'For you,' he said. 'It's Jacques.'

Lesley did smile, then, more to assure Matt's annoyance than because she felt thrilled by the call. Dealing with Jacques was not going to be easy right now.

'Hello,' she said cautiously.

'He still there?' Jacques asked without preamble.

'Yes.' Lesley was aware that Matt's slow smile had vanished and that he was listening to every word.

'Damn!' Jacques heaved a sigh. 'So did you "handle" it?'

'After a fashion.'

'What does that mean?'

Lesley felt Matt's glittering dark eyes on her. 'I'll explain later.'

'He's listening,' Jacques guessed.

'Yes.'

'Oh. How about I pick you up? We can go for a drive. Talk?'

And there was an avoidance-avoidance conflict for you, Lesley thought grimly. Go out and be grilled by Jacques, or stay at home and be glared at by Matt. She weighed the alternatives. 'I guess.'

'Such enthusiasm!' Jacques chided her.

She made a small guilty noise. 'I'm sorry. I——'

'Forget it. I'll be there at seven-fifteen.' He rang off before she could say another word.

She hung the phone up and walked back to her chair, all the while aware of Matt's eyes on her. Harry began determinedly talking about a series of articles he was going to do on the flotsam and jetsam that washed up on Maine beaches. Neither Matt nor Lesley heard a word. He looked at her accusingly throughout the rest of the meal; Lesley didn't look at him at all.

The drive with Jacques was as fraught with tension as she had expected it to be.

'When's he leaving?' Jacques wanted to know the second she slipped into the car.

'When are you coming back?' was the last question Matt had asked her as she'd walked out of the door.

'I don't know,' she said now, just as she'd said then. 'I haven't any idea.'

Jacques didn't seem any more pleased with her answer than Matt had been. The encounter went downhill from there. Jacques drove north along the coast road, and the scenery was lovely in the twilight, but neither of them noticed a bit of it. They were each too aware of their own thoughts to notice anything else. Jacques, Lesley knew, wanted the assurance that his proposal had been accepted, that the divorce was under way, that their future together was guaranteed. And Lesley couldn't give it to him.

'Why not?' Jacques demanded when he finally pulled over to the side of the road and they sat in his car, overlooking the sea.

Lesley shook her head wearily. 'I just can't.'

'He wants you back.'

She sighed. 'He says he does.'

Jacques slammed his fist on the dashboard. 'And you're just going to knuckle under? Give in?'

'I am not going to knuckle under!' Lesley flared.

'What do you call it, then?' He glowered at her.

'Look,' Lesley said finally, 'there's no way I'm going to be able to make you understand. I don't understand everything myself. I—let's just forget Matt for a while. He's not the centre of the universe.'

Jacques gave her a dark look. 'Isn't he?'

Her fingers knotted in her lap. 'I want to go home.'

For a long moment Jacques didn't move. Then he sighed heavily and raked his fingers through his hair. 'Damn it, Lesley, I don't want to drive you away from me. I don't want it to be like this.'

She reached over and touched his arm. 'I know.'

He turned to her, his face anguished. 'How can you——?' He broke off, seeing equal anguish in hers. 'Hell, all right, I'll take you home.'

Jerkily he put the car into reverse and backed around out of the overlook and on to the highway. By the time he pulled up in front of Lesley's house again, he had managed to dredge up a reasonable facsimile of a smile.

'I don't like it,' he told her with a wry grimace, 'but I guess I can put up with it. Maybe I can even understand.' He sighed and shifted in the seat of the car. 'You've been through a lot of pressure this past year or so. You didn't even know if Colter was dead or alive a good part of the time. I guess you should have time to sort him out before you say goodbye.' He touched her cheek gently. 'Right?'

'Right,' Lesley agreed, giving him a wan smile and getting out of the car. But, as she went up the steps and into the house, she couldn't have said if it made sense or not.

The tapping on her bedroom door startled her. She hadn't been asleep, of course. Sleep had been hard to come by. In her mind she had played over all the conversations she'd had with Matt since he had come back, drifting on memories, buffeted about by waves of longing and dreams unfulfilled. The rhythmic noise brought her back to reality with a jerk.

'Harry?' she called softly. It wouldn't be either of the children, she was certain. Doors didn't slow them down for a second.

'It's me,' came the muffled reply.

Lesley jerked up. Matt? He hadn't spoken to her since supper. He had glared at her when she'd left with Jacques, but Harry had distracted him so that he couldn't intervene without being rude. And when she'd come back, he had been on the porch still talking to Harry. She had decided not to join them. It was 'man talk', she had convinced herself, and they wouldn't appreciate the interruption. So she'd taken the opportunity to avoid him.

But she couldn't avoid him now.

Reaching for her robe and hauling it on, she went to the door, opening it a crack, and found herself staring into a bare chest. She swallowed hard. 'What do you want?'

'Have you got any gauze?'

She blinked. 'Gauze?'

'Bandage. I can't find any.'

She opened the door further, concerned. 'What's wrong?'

He grimaced. 'No big deal. I have to change the dressing on my leg.'

'Oh.' She felt stupid and self-conscious, wrapping the robe more tightly around her. 'I have Telfa pads. I'll get some.' She moved to go past him.

'I've already looked in the medicine cabinet,' he told her.

'They're in the linen closet.' She flipped on the hall light and rummaged through the closet, at last finding the box. She offered it to him, along with a roll of tape. 'I have more in my bag downstairs.'

'This is fine. Thanks.' He took them from her, their fingers touching, the heat of his making hers burn.

For a moment they stood staring at each other—Lesley mesmerised by the sight of him bare-chested, cheeks flushed, the button of his jeans already undone; and Matthew, licking parched lips, obviously entranced with the sleep-rumpled woman before him. Then the moment passed, and Lesley recollected herself, backing quickly away.

Matt gave her a mocking look, which flustered her even more. Then he moved to go past her towards the bathroom.

Whew! Lesley thought, and started back to her room, then stopped. She turned, staring after him, suddenly indecisive. In her mind's eye she saw more than the bare chest and undeniable masculinity. What she recalled was the high colour that ran along his cheekbones, the parched lips, and the heat of his hand when their fingers had briefly touched.

Biting her lip, she went back down the hall and knocked on the bathroom door. 'Matt?'

The door opened and he looked down at her. She was right about the hectic colour, and she noted how white he was around the mouth. But, at the same time as she saw it, she saw the uncompromising set of his jaw and the thin line of his lips.

'Are you . . . I mean . . . I thought you might need some help.'

Dark eyes considered her curiously, then he pressed his lips together and exhaled slowly. 'I might,' he allowed.

'I would . . . help you,' she ventured hesitantly.

'Oh yes?' He sounded half wary, half sarcastic.

Lesley dredged up all her courage. 'Really.'

He shrugged, then opened the door further, letting her in.

During the first months of their marriage, he had been shot while covering a story in Guyana. It had been a flesh wound, nothing serious, really, but another few inches and he could have died. The thought had terrified her, and she had let him know as soon as he got off the plane. She had harped on it later at the hospital, and still later when she had him at home. He had lost patience with her entirely.

'I'm all right!' he had shouted at her. 'Stop fussing, for heaven's sake!'

This time she wouldn't fuss, Lesley promised herself. She would be clinical and detached, betraying no feelings at all.

It was a terrific theory. But, like a lot of terrific theories, in reality it didn't work.

She found that out the moment he dropped his jeans.

Her mind reeled. Matthew Colter clad only in briefs and

a bandage was hard to remain impervious to. However willing the spirit was, the flesh was definitely weakening.

Sucking in an unsteady breath, she knelt on the small round rug and began, with nerveless fingers, to strip the bandage from his thigh.

Matt stood his ground under her touch, but she felt him tense as she peeled away the layers of gauze, and he couldn't disguise his wince when the last of it pulled away to bare the red, still oozing wound.

Lesley grimaced, her fears realised. 'How long has it been infected like this?' she demanded.

Matt shrugged, glancing over his shoulder to where she knelt behind him. 'It's always oozed. There's a drain in it.'

'Yes, I see that. You need it changed.' She touched the skin near the wound itself. 'It feels hot. And you've had a fever. Aren't you on antibiotics?'

'I was.'

'They're gone?'

'I . . . didn't bring them.'

'What?' She stared at him, aghast.

He shrugged again. 'When I left Becca's, I . . . didn't exactly plan it. I just . . . left. Went out for a newspaper on Friday night and . . . didn't go back.' He glared down at her defiantly.

'You brought a duffel bag.'

'K-Mart special. I picked up a toothbrush, deodorant, jeans and shirts. I didn't have anything there worth going back for.'

Not even Becca? Lesley wanted to ask. 'Not even your antibiotics?' she said.

'I was getting better.'

'You're not now. And you won't unless you get back on something right away. What were you taking?'

She wasn't surprised that he knew. It was like Matt to be observant, just as it was like him to be careless with his health.

'I can get you some more in the morning,' she told him.

'Dr Payson will prescribe it.'

'I won't have to see him?'

'He'll have to change the drain.'

'I won't go into a hospital!' He was adamant.

'I don't imagine you'll have to. Now hold still, so I can take care of this tonight. The dressing at least should have been changed long before this.'

'I couldn't do it myself.'

'I can see that. You should have asked——' She broke off before she could say, 'me'.

Matt gave her a mocking look. 'I didn't know you'd be so willing.'

Lesley's lips pressed together in a thin, tight line. She made no rejoinder, instead forcing herself to concentrate on the task at hand. She popped a thermometer into his mouth, forestalling any further comments on his part. And, when he was silent, she cleaned his wound with soap and water, then daubed it with an antibiotic ointment she had to hand, and finally rebandaged it carefully, all the time refusing to let herself think about the feel of Matt's thigh beneath her fingers or about the situation that he had been in when he had received this wound.

When at last she went to stand up, she found she had been holding her breath. Letting it out slowly, she locked her fingers together to hide their trembling.

'Much obliged,' Matthew said around the thermometer, hauling his jeans back up and zipping them.

'It was . . . nothing,' Lesley lied, her cheeks still warm, her fingers tingling from having brushed against the heated flesh of his leg. She snatched the thermometer from his mouth.

'Was it, Les?' he asked softly. 'Nothing, I mean?'

She opened the door quickly and backed out, not daring an answer. 'I'll give Dr Payson a ring in the morning. Goodnight.'

Matt gave her a smile that was tender, painful, and totally haunting.

'Sweet dreams,' he said to her back.

CHAPTER FIVE

SWEET dreams? Not likely—at least, not that night.

But, as one day turned into the next, it sometimes seemed to Lesley that her dreams were the only pleasant part of her life. Matt's return had pitched her headlong into such a morass of emotional confusion that sleep became her only refuge. There everything was clear; but it grew muddled again the moment she woke up.

Outwardly much of her life showed no signs of change. Bright and early on Monday morning, she went back to school just as if she hadn't spent the weekend in an emotional tailspin. She gave eye exams, checked hearing, patched scrapes and took slivers out of grubby hands. She said not a word about the man at home asleep in Teddy's other bed. On Tuesday she did approximately the same, as well as sewing a fairy costume for Rita to wear in the Brownies' skit on Wednesday night, and helped Teddy with his current events—tried to help Teddy with his current events, actually. But she wasn't much good at explaining the stock-market fluctuations to a ten-year-old, and she got even worse with Matt sitting right there, listening.

Finally he said, 'I'll explain it,' and, since that was preferable to having him sit there listening while she tried to, she shrugged and let him.

But, whatever she did, Matt was never far away.

Never far away? That was putting it mildly. Underfoot, more like. He watched her bake, then offered to help stir. He watched her read, then read her articles out of the paper in his hand. He told stories to Rita, explained rocket launchings and long division to Teddy, proof-read Uncle Harry's articles, dried dishes and fed the cat.

Both nights she changed the dressing on his leg, all the while trying to steel herself against the feelings that assailed her as her fingers touched the warm, resilient flesh of his thigh. It wasn't easy, and Matt made it less so by shifting beneath the touch of her fingers and watching her every move with a flushed face and an arousal that he made no attempt to hide.

On Wednesday she came home from school, crossing her fingers that today wouldn't be like the past two days. She needed some respite. Every waking moment she'd been aware of him. When she was working or driving from school to school, he was in her thoughts. She couldn't go on like this.

Surely he would get bored soon? Lesley thought. And when he got bored, he would do what he'd always done—he would leave.

But, 'I'm not bored,' Matt said when she'd intimated as much as she got ready to go to school that morning.

'You intend to make a career out of drying dishes and feeding the cat?'

He looked up from where he sat at the kitchen table. 'Do you?'

'Of course not!'

'But it's part of what you do,' he said mildly.

'Yes, but——'

'So I'm doing it too. Don't worry, I'll keep busy. I'm helping Harry on the paper, writing for him.'

Lesley gave him a sceptical look. 'Matt Colter writing for a minuscule Maine weekly?'

'There are more important things in life than being on the cutting edge of world news,' he told her gruffly. 'Besides, you make your own quality. I'll make mine with Harry.'

'Says who?'

'Says me.'

She sniffed doubtfully. 'Now,' she allowed. But he would change his tune soon enough, she was certain. Just let opportunity knock, and she was sure he would be out of the door without ever looking back.

And she thought the time had come that afternoon as she turned off the lane into their long winding drive, and, rounding the bend, spied two news vans camped in front of the house.

She slowed, then slithered to a stop, astonished when five people with cameras, notepads and paraphernalia she didn't even recognise descended upon her.

'Mrs Colter, are you——?'

'Mrs Colter, is your husband——?'

'You are Mrs Colter, aren't you?'

The questions flew thick and furious, and Lesley, half out of the car, seriously considered climbing back in and locking the doors. What on earth were they talking to her for? Where the devil was Matt?

She glanced up at the house, expecting to see another dozen or so people surrounding him. She saw no one, least of all Matt. So much for her theory that the moment he got a chance for contact with his old cronies again he would be raring to go.

Odd, she would have thought he would eat this sort of attention up. But then, ever since his escape, he'd been avoiding it. There had been plenty of interviews with the other escaped hostages, but none with him.

Obviously he was still avoiding them now, perhaps in the hope that, if he didn't appear, they would go away. Fat chance, Lesley thought. This bunch was clearly as persistent as Matt Colter himself. If they weren't going to get it from him, they seemed determined to get it from her.

She grimaced, steeling herself for the confrontation, knowing that, unless she planned on sitting in the car all night, there was no way out but through them. Sighing, she unlocked and opened the door of the car.

'What's he doing here, Mrs Colter?' a short, bushy-bearded man asked her.

'Is it true he's under psychiatric care?'

'Did he have his leg amputated?'

'When's he going back to work?'

More questions—all impertinent, all pushy. Lesley wrapped her arms against her chest and prepared to bull her way through the horde. She would have dearly loved to push back. She didn't because she knew how wild the stories could get then. But she didn't know quite what else to do either, come to that.

Fortunately she didn't have to do anything. Quite suddenly, above the babble of questions, another voice spoke with strong authority. 'Let my wife alone.'

Half a dozen heads swung around to see Matt, his hands in his pockets, his feet planted firmly on the top step. The group parted and Lesley plunged through, climbing up the path and then up the steps, her eyes fastened on Matt the whole way.

The antibiotics she had got him from Dr Payson had gone a long way towards controlling the infection, and he no longer had that high feverish flush along his cheekbones. Now he looked pale and still gaunt, but determined. He met her gaze only for a fleeting instant as he reached out and took her arm, drawing her up next to him and into the crook of his shoulder. Lesley nestled there by instinct, slipping an arm around his waist, noting as she did so that the cameraman was shooting.

'So what gives, Colter?' the bushy-bearded fellow demanded. 'Doorbell broken?'

'I was busy.'

'Well, we won't take much of your time. We've heard from just about everyone else about how you masterminded the escape. Now we want to hear it from you.'

Lesley turned slightly in the hold he had on her, lifting her gaze to watch his face.

'I've got nothing to say.'

'You must have something. Everyone says you were the brains behind it, the master planner, the executioner, as it were,' the man went on.

Matt's fingers tightened on her arm.

'A regular bona-fide hero,' bushy-beard continued.

'No.'

Bushy-beard blinked. 'No? No what?'

'No, it wasn't heroic.' Matt's voice was cold and hoarse.
Lesley thought he sounded suddenly as if he hadn't spoken
in years. He licked his lips, then swallowed hard. 'I
hope . . . that anyone . . . would have done the same.'

Bushy-beard shook his head at this modesty. 'Daring, I'd
say. First-rate thriller material. Drugged your captors,
Griswald told us. How did you manage it?'

Lesley saw Matt's jaw tighten. For a moment it didn't
seem as if he would answer at all. He glared at the camera
whirling away, then seemed to make up his mind. At last he
spoke one word, and even that sounded as if it had been
dragged up from his toes. 'Force.'

The red-haired woman, who had remained silent, now
spoke up. 'You forced someone to help you?' she prompted.

But that one word was all they were going to get. Lesley
felt Matt's muscles bunching and tightening, saw his feet
shift on the step. His eyes flickered around almost wildly,
seeking escape, as if this captivity was worse than the one he
had escaped. It was so unlike his usually unflappable on-
camera behaviour that Lesley drew in a worried breath.

Apparently the fact that Matt was about to bolt
communicated itself to his bushy-bearded inquisitor, for the
man abruptly changed his tack, mounting the steps, smiling
and clapping Matt on the back. 'Well, I'd call it true
heroism—any way you look at it. Four men captive, four
men free, and only you wounded. No casualties at all,' he
said as he turned and faced the camera.

'A boy died,' Matt said bluntly.

'A boy?' Bushy-beard sounded puzzled for a moment,
then brightened. 'Oh, yes—the kid zealot. The one who ran
after you to haul you back. Hamish Al-something-or-other.
One of the terrorists,' he added dismissively as a postscript.

There was a pause, and Lesley saw a look of pain on

Matt's face so stark and yet so fleeting that she thought she must have imagined it. His whole being clenched and then he consciously seemed to make himself relax. Shrugging his shoulders slightly, he said with cool indifference, 'Just as you say. One of the terrorists.'

Then, abruptly, he turned and, taking Lesley with him, he walked into the house, shutting the door firmly behind them.

'Are you——?' Lesley began worriedly.

'I'm fine,' he snapped, pacing around the room, raking his fingers through his hair.

'You don't look——'

'I said I'm fine. Leave me alone.' He bit the words out and took the stairs two at a time, making Lesley wince at the pain he must have inflicted on his leg.

That was fine?

The doorbell was ringing again.

She opened the door. 'He doesn't have anything else to say,' she told them.

'But——'

'You've got a story. You talked to him. What more do you want?'

'When's he coming back?' the red-headed woman asked her.

'When's he going back to work?' Four upturned faces stared at her.

'He says he's not,' Lesley replied quietly.

Bushy-beard stuck a microphone right in her face. 'Do you believe that?'

'That's what he says.' And Lesley shut the door and leaned back against it, unsure whether she believed it or not.

The news teams were every bit as persistent as Lesley had figured they would be. Matt hadn't given them much of a story, she had given even less. So they went to see what they could find in the town. The next day everyone from the mayor to the town drunk was given an opportunity to express an opinion about Matt Colter.

The town, God bless it, protected him as if he were one of its own. Speculate as they might in private—and Lesley knew they were speculating quite a bit—everyone was as close as a clam for the Press. What happened in Day's Harbor, Maine, was nobody's business but Day's Harbor's own.

'Matt Colter?' Old Barney at the general store looked at the bushy-bearded newsman as if, were he to think long and hard, he might just vaguely place the name. 'Ayuh, I know 'im. Nice feller.' And that was that.

'Colters? Lovely people,' the postmistress told the red-headed woman. 'The finest kind, him and his wife. Them two children.' She nodded, smiling. 'Good folks.'

They met similar reticence elsewhere, and fortunately they missed talking to Jacques.

Lesley wasn't surprised at their attitude. Matt was.

'What am I to them?' he wondered aloud as they sat in the front room late in the week and read the news weeklies' accounts of their unsatisfactory interviews.

'Her husband,' Harry said bluntly with a nod in Lesley's direction.

Lesley looked up, startled to find Matt staring at her consideringly. 'I'm glad someone realises it,' he said.

But Lesley was still afraid even to think it, though Matt gave all indications of sticking around. Not only had he emphatically turned away the newscasters she'd imagined he would be delighted to see, he had spent the entire day in the office with Harry.

'Doing what?' Lesley asked him.

'Writing stories based on wire service reports.'

'Matt Colter? Depend on wire service?' she scoffed as she picked up a pile of charts she needed to update. 'Why read about trouble in Belfast when in seven short hours you can be there?'

'I don't want to be there, Lesley,' he said evenly, meeting

her gaze squarely. 'I want to be here.'

She had to admit that he did more than pay lip service to the notion too. Every day he spent time with the children, behaving like the sort of father she had once dreamed he would be. And he genuinely seemed to enjoy it too. Sometimes she even had to pinch herself to be sure she was awake and not just dreaming.

But, though his behaviour was everything she would have once wished, it didn't make her happy. It made her tense. She watched Teddy and Rita develop their attachment to him, she watched Teddy's hero-worship grow and Rita's enthusiasm increase, and she grew angry.

She saw herself in both of them. They were falling under the very same spell she had once fallen under. They idolised Matt, hurried home from school to be with him, followed him around with the devotion of new-born ducklings, and Matt encouraged it, just the way he had once encouraged her.

But what could she say? Don't? He'll hurt you the same way he hurt me? He'll leave you the same way he left me?

They wouldn't believe her.

'Teddy and I are going to Ferris's after school to see Robby's rocket,' Matt said to her as she bandaged his leg that evening.

Lesley sucked in her breath. 'Why?' she asked harshly.

Matt looked over his shoulder at her. 'Because he wants to.'

'And you always do what Teddy wants?' she demanded.

He frowned. 'Not always, no. But in this case, why not?'

She slapped a piece of gauze over his nearly healed wound so hard that he winced. 'You'll hurt him,' she muttered.

'Hurt him?'

She pressed her lips together. 'Don't go innocent on me. I know you, remember?'

'Do you?' said Matt. 'I wonder. I won't hurt him, Lesley. How could I hurt him.'

She bent her head. 'Leaving him.'

'I've already told you, I won't.'

'And you never have before, of course,' she retorted bitterly, strapping the gauze down with surgical tape.

He rolled over and braced himself on his elbows, glowering at her. 'You still don't believe me, do you?'

'No, I don't. I *can't.*'

His jaw clenched. 'Afraid, Les?' he taunted.

She only had to look at the six feet of blatant masculinity sprawled on the bed wearing only his briefs and she knew the answer to that. 'Just don't hurt him,' she said fiercely. 'Just *don't!*' And she turned and fled, the blood pounding in her veins.

Whatever she told him, and whatever he felt, Lesley discovered when she got home from school the next day that Matt and Teddy had, indeed, visited Robby and his dad to check out the rocket.

Teddy ran to meet her when she got out of the car just before dinner time; he was full of enthusiasm, bubbling over with the wonders of the rocket that Robby and his father had built and about the impromptu game of five hundred that Matt and Robby's dad had played with them.

Lesley, who'd had a hard day, barely attended to his chatter, except to note that he was even more excited than ever. And he would have further to fall, she thought bitterly. He had been doing fine before Matt had come on to the scene. Damn Matt, anyway.

'That's nice, Teddy,' she said, cutting him off mid-sentence. 'Now, go and get your homework done before supper.'

Teddy's face fell, but when she didn't give an inch he went. But he returned undaunted when the meal was on the table.

'It really was neat, Mama,' he began, as he slid on to a chair and began shovelling potatoes on to his plate.

'What was?' Lesley asked absently. 'You're sitting over here, Rita,' she told her daughter who had just come into the kitchen.

'But I wanna sit by Matt,' Rita argued. 'It's my turn.'

'The rocket was neat,' Teddy went on, 'and it's my turn,' he told his sister. 'You sit over there.' He indicated the chair next to their mother.

'Huh—uh——' Rita began to wail.

Before Matt had come back they had argued over who could sit next to Lesley.

'Rita!' Lesley said sharply. 'Sit down.'

'But, Mama——'

'Sit down, Rita.' Matt's voice was quiet, but firm. Rita's lower lip jutted out, but after a moment, when her pout got no sympathy from him, she took her place next to her mother. Lesley sucked in a sharp breath.

'. . . an' Matt says we can make one too,' Teddy went on doggedly, passing Uncle Harry the beans without taking any himself.

Matt's brows went up and he fixed Teddy with a hard stare. Teddy hastily pulled the bowl of beans back and heaped some on his plate.

'Make one what?' Lesley tried to follow the conversation through growing irritation. *She* would have told Teddy to take some beans. Matt didn't have to interfere.

'Make a rocket. Like the one Robby and his dad made,' Teddy said patiently.

'A rocket?' Lesley asked, finally focusing entirely on what the boy was saying.

Teddy nodded, oblivious to maternal concerns. 'Yeah.'

'They're dangerous.'

'Not really. Dad says they're not. Dad says it isn't hard to build 'em. We could do it together and set it off—Dad says so.'

Lesley fixed Matt with a hard look. 'He does, does he?' she challenged him.

Matt met her gaze with a level one of his own. 'Yes, he does.'

For a moment a private battle raged. Two pairs of eyes duelled harshly. Then, when Matt didn't back down,

Lesley turned to her own son. 'And will he bandage you up when you're blown to smithereens, I wonder?' she asked sweetly.

Teddy paused, his fork half-way to his mouth. 'What's smith-er-eens?' he asked, his grasp of English still not up to coping with every colloquialism.

'Pieces,' Lesley said bluntly. She fixed her gaze on Matt, anger fuelling her words. 'Haven't you had your fill of bloodshed yet?' she demanded. 'I should have thought you wouldn't have to resort to killing a child.'

Matt's face went absolutely white.

For what seemed an eternity, not a sound was heard. Then abruptly he shoved back his chair, stood, and stalked out of the house.

She had gone too far, and she knew it. 'I didn't mean——' she called after him. But a second later the back door slammed shut.

'I really didn't——' She looked around the table, helpless, confused, embarrassed at the accusing looks she got from the children, from Uncle Harry.

'He wasn't gonna kill me, Mama,' Teddy told her stolidly.

'No, I—I . . . know that.' Lesley was still staring, stunned, at the door Matt had walked out of. If she ran after him, chances were she would only make things worse. But if she stayed here . . .

'Pass the beans,' Uncle Harry said to Teddy.

'But——'

Uncle Harry's brows lifted. 'Pass the beans, Ted. It's not for you to be worrying.'

'But——'

'Your mother will take care of it.'

'But——'

'The beans, Teddy.'

Teddy passed the beans.

Matt didn't come back for supper, and he didn't come back afterwards either. Teddy did his maths homework without Matt's encouragement. Rita studied her spelling words with Uncle Harry under protest, keeping her eye on the door all the while. They put the dishes in the dishwasher, had baths, and got into bed, and still Matt hadn't come back.

'I need him to kiss me goodnight,' Rita said as she curled up under the blankets and scowled at Lesley.

'He will,' Lesley promised, crossing her fingers in hopes that she wasn't lying.

'Really?'

'Really.'

'You're sure?'

'Yes,' Lesley said firmly, giving Rita a kiss herself. 'Goodnight.'

'You shouldn'a said that to him,' Teddy told his mother when she came to shut off his light.

Lesley, who knew that already, didn't reply.

'D'you think he'll go away for good?'

She didn't know what to say to that.

'I don't want him to,' Teddy told her. 'I really like him.'

'Yes,' Lesley said softly, brushing her lips across his, giving him a faint, worried smile. *I was afraid you might*.

'He's still not back,' Uncle Harry told her when she came back downstairs.

Lesley shrugged, trying for more complacency than she felt. 'He's a big boy. I'm sure he'll be fine.'

Harry's brows rose again, displaying his very obvious scepticism. 'Not too familiar with these parts, though, I don't reckon,' he commented, rustling his newspaper in discontent.

Lesley's lips compressed, recognising a guilt-trip when it was offered. 'I suppose you think it's my fault.'

'Didn't say that.'

'You think I should go and look for him, though.'

'Wouldn't hurt.'

'I didn't *make* him go!'

Bushy white brows rode up even higher.

Lesley scowled. 'It's only nine-forty-five.'

'And dark as pitch.'

'There's a moon tonight.'

'And a sky full of clouds coverin' it up.'

'You really are worried about him?'

Harry fixed her with a steady stare. 'Aren't you?'

Lesley twisted her hands together, telling herself she wasn't, knowing, in fact, she was. 'I guess so.'

Harry smiled then, a gentle, hopeful smile. 'Then go, sweetheart. Look for him.'

'And if I find him?'

'Bring him home.'

Three simple words. If she'd ever been able to do that, none of the last two and a half years would ever have happened. But she hadn't because she had never had that much influence over Matt Colter. She had never mattered that much in his life.

And now?

Don't be ridiculous, she chided herself. You're not going after him with the intention of repairing a broken marriage, you're only trying to keep him from breaking his fool neck.

The Maine night was cold and damp, the breeze off the ocean mingling the smells of sea and mud as it lifted Lesley's hair. She shivered as she picked her way along.

She checked the docks, then walked along the main street of town, because, she told herself, those were the logical places to look for him first. They were also, if she was honest, places where she had hoped to find Matthew. She hadn't.

That left the point. She sighed, staring south-east towards the narrow strip of land which ended at the old stone lighthouse. Why, Matthew? she asked him silently. Why there? There were too many memories out there. Too many broken hopes and shattered expectations.

But where else? She cast a longing gaze back towards town, towards the house on the hill where Uncle Harry sat snug and warm, waiting. Maybe, she thought, Matt was already back there, snug and warm with him.

But he wasn't, she knew. She would have passed him if he had headed back. Reluctantly, then, she headed out along the trail that ran away from the road through the spruce and pine trees that crowded the narrow promontory.

There was, of course, no guarantee she would find him there, either. But there was, she knew, a better than even chance.

Before their marriage she and Matt had spent a lot of time on the point, sitting and staring out towards the horizon, their arms wrapped around each other until the lure of the horizon paled against the lure of their bodies pressed together.

Pushing away the memory, Lesley hurried on, her feet slipping as she picked her way along the moist, mossy, needle-covered ground. Uncle Harry was right: Matt could easily lose his way up here and, with his still mending leg, he might trip, get hurt. She debated calling his name, then wondered if he would answer if he heard.

He had been angry when he'd left—at her, certainly. But there was more to it than that, Lesley was sure. Her comment had been petty and thoughtless, the product of irritation and anger of her own. But it had been no worse than any other sharp remark she had made to him since he'd returned. Those he had fended off, retorting with cutting remarks of his own. This one had, for reasons unknown, cut him to the core.

Lesley had nearly reached the end of the trail, where the trees gave way to the rocky tip of the point, when she found him.

He was sitting on the rocks just beyond the lighthouse, staring down at his feet, his elbows on his knees. A cigarette dangled from his fingers. As Lesley watched silently, he took a long draw on it, then rested his forehead against his fist. This was a Matthew she had never seen before. His head was bent, his shoulders slumped. He had 'defeat' written all over him.

It didn't matter that half the time she hated him. It didn't matter that she no longer trusted him. She only wanted to go to him, take away his problems, soothe and comfort him. At the same time, she recognised that she had no idea what his problem was.

She took a step forward, loosening a rock with her shoe, causing it to tumble down the side of the cliff. At the sound, Matt looked around. Seeing her, he straightened up, stubbing out the cigarette. The slump vanished, and he stood up.

'Afraid I got lost?' he asked mockingly.

So much for sympathy, Lesley thought. 'Harry was.'

'Ah—figures.' He started to go past her, but she caught his arm.

'I'm sorry,' she said quickly, needing to.

Matt stopped. 'Sorry?' He looked down at her, frowning.

'For . . . what I said . . . about . . . about . . .'

'Oh, that,' he said dismissively. 'No sweat. Don't worry about it—you've said worse.' But she heard a trace of roughness in his voice when he spoke. He started to brush past her again, but she didn't let go.

'Really, Matt, I didn't mean . . .'

'I said, forget it!' He shook her hand off and was past her in an instant, striding towards the road.

'Matt!' She hurried after him. 'Matthew!'

He spun around, glaring at her. 'What?'

'What happened to you?' The question was out before she could stop it, rephrase it, reconsider it.

He stood stock still. It seemed to Lesley that he wasn't even breathing. Their eyes met again, and now, even in the darkness, she could see anguish in them. He had the look of a wounded buck shot by a hunter, the look of a man at odds with a world in which he was just about to die. It was so unlike the usual stoic, untouched Matt Colter that she almost could not believe it.

He swallowed convulsively, then his eyes wavered and

lowered. Lesley took a cautious step towards him as if, were she to move swiftly, he, like the buck, would bolt. He didn't. He stood his ground, but the tension in him made the very air around him vibrate. Another step brought her close enough to see a faint sheen of perspiration on his upper lip, across his cheekbones and forehead.

'What's the matter?' she persisted.

'Nothing.'

'Is it the fever again?'

He hesitated, then nodded almost jerkily. 'Yeah, I expect it is.'

It wasn't the fever that had sent him running, but it seemed all the answer she was going to get. Guiltily, she shook her head. 'You shouldn't have stayed out. I am sorry.'

He shrugged awkwardly.

She took another step and then another, coming alongside him. Warily she reached out and touched his forehead. It was cool, despite the way he looked. The infection seemed to be leaving, but he still looked dreadful. 'You ought to get some more sleep.'

He let out a ragged sigh, then a rough, harsh-sounding laugh. 'Ain't it the truth?'

Lesley knew what he meant. That first night wasn't the only time she had heard him downstairs since he'd come. Most nights, in fact, footsteps prowled below while the rest of the house slept. She had mentioned it to Dr Payson and he had shaken his head.

'Not unusual,' he'd said. 'But not good for him, either.'

'Come on,' she said to Matt now. 'Let's go home.' She moved ahead of him, concentrating merely on getting him to come with her, not letting herself think beyond that. She willed him to fall in with her, and was relieved when, after a long moment's hesitation, he did.

They walked in silence, their arms brushing briefly when the path narrowed. They reached the road at last, climbing over the rail and keeping to the shoulder as they wound their way back towards town.

'Did Harry really make you come after me?' Matt asked suddenly.

'He suggested it.'

'You wouldn't have otherwise.' His voice was bitter.

'I . . . don't know. I might have. I felt . . . guilty.'

'Guilty?'

'What I said . . . it wasn't kind. I didn't expect you to take it so . . .'

'Personally?' He gave her a sardonic look.

'Well, yes.' She slanted a glance up at him. 'I mean, I never meant to hurt . . . Did it . . .? Are you . . .?' But she couldn't frame a question to save her life.

'It didn't,' Matt mocked. 'And I'm not. I'm fine.'

But he didn't sound fine even now.

'You shouldn't have come out alone. You don't know the area.'

'I know the point. I could have got there blindfolded. I thought about it so long. I——' He broke off suddenly, shrugging as if what he had been about to say didn't matter. 'We went there plenty of times, if you remember,' he finished casually.

She had never been able to forget. 'You might have hurt your leg,' she persisted.

'It's getting better. Takes a while to get back to normal.' He grimaced. 'The guy at the hospital said it would be good as new. Said all of me would be, eventually.' His ironic laugh told her he doubted it.

'If you get some rest, maybe,' Lesley concurred as they approached the house.

'I guess.'

Lesley slowed her pace slightly, suddenly less willing to be rid of him. They were talking to each other at last—albeit in bits and pieces—not just sniping, which they had been doing almost since he had come through the door.

She was finding this new, touchier, less invincible, more vulnerable Matt Colter intriguing, and as they turned to walk up the drive she couldn't help counselling, 'You ought to try sleeping a bit more tonight.'

Matt gave her an oblique glance, then concentrated on the light in the house ahead. 'Yeah,' he said, 'I will.' He gave her a bleak smile as he stopped at the top of the walk.

She paused a moment, thinking of a thousand things to say, afraid to say any of them. 'Aren't you coming in?' she asked finally.

'In a bit.' He reached into his jacket pocket and took out his cigarettes. 'I've got some thinking to do. 'Night,' he said, and apparently that meant she was dismissed.

''Night,' said Lesley, but, when she closed the door between them, emotionally she hadn't left him at all.

He wasn't the same man she had married—she knew that now. Gone was the impregnable self-assurance, the tough ego, and the indestructible shell that had made him the intrepid reporter she had married. In his place there was a new man—a new Matt Colter—a man she really didn't know at all.

He was an enigma to her, a puzzle, a tantalising, intriguing jigsaw of a man. And, despite her better judgement, she itched to try to put together the pieces. She just didn't know if she dared.

Once before she and Matthew had put together a relationship: once before it had smashed into a million pieces. Was there any point in trying to do it again?

The possibility tempted her, taunted her.

She found herself wondering about it—about him—at all hours. She went to bed wondering that night. She woke at three, still wondering, and saw the light on downstairs.

She didn't investigate. She knew who it was now. And if Harry was up too—well, they could keep each other company. If she went down, she didn't know what would happen.

She didn't know what she *wanted* to happen. And, until she was sure, she was keeping her distance.

CHAPTER SIX

EASIER said than done, she found.

Matt was everywhere. And, while she did her best to avoid him most times, it wasn't as easy as simply taking Rita and disappearing for a day of shopping in Freeport. It meant avoiding spending time with her children, avoiding time with Harry, avoiding the leisurely evenings she had been wont to spend simply sitting in the living-room enjoying a good book or a television programme.

And, while she could do all that—and did—for a time, what she couldn't avoid was the effect he was having on her heart.

She tried not to let him know it. It seemed the only defence she had. But it got harder and harder to tell herself he was leaving again, when every day he seemed more deeply entrenched in their lives.

May turned into June. The raw, oozing flesh on Matt's thigh turned into new pink skin and scar tissue. The phone calls from sensationalist magazines stopped, while legitimate calls from his editors increased. And Matt stayed right where he was.

But, although he stayed, he still looked burnt out, haunted, and a far cry from the man Lesley once knew. Time and again Lesley was tempted to confront him, to question him, but every time they spoke tension rippled in the air between them, and she could never find the words. If she asked, if she showed that she cared, she knew it would mean that her guard was slipping, that she was, against all good sense, letting him know he mattered still. She got to looking haunted too.

People commented on it. At one school the principal told her she looked as if she had the flu that was attacking the students. At another the secretary wondered aloud if Lesley was getting proper rest. She wasn't. And she would have liked nothing better than to go home and curl up in her bed and sleep for hours, but thoughts of Matt wouldn't let her. And today neither would the nursing association meeting that was going to be held in Portland that night.

Sighing, Lesley dragged herself up the steps and dumped an armload of end-of-the-school-year paperwork on to the kitchen table. At least, she told herself, she would have a legitimate evening away from Matt.

She didn't count on his being in the kitchen when she came back down from getting cleaned up and changing into a clean summer dress before she prepared to leave.

He took in the fresh clothes and the purposeful gathering up of briefcase and notes, and asked, 'Where are you going now?'

'Portland.'

'Portland?' He scowled. 'Isn't that a little drastic just to avoid me?'

'I'm not avoiding you,' she said, stooping to put on her heels. Not precisely true, but tonight she would have been driving to Portland in any case.

'No?'

'No. I have a nursing association meeting there.'

'Can't you miss it?'

Lesley stared.

'Well, can't you?'

'This from the man who flew into the face of speeding bullets to get a story?'

Matt raked his fingers through his hair. 'Forget that.'

Lesley shrugged. 'No, I can't miss it,' she said finally. 'I have to speak.'

'I'll come along.'

Her head jerked up. 'What?'

'I'll drive you.'

'No!'

'I thought you weren't avoiding me,' he reminded her silkily.

'I'm not.'

'Well then . . .'

'It's pointless. I don't need a driver. I——'

'I want to come.' His tone brooked no opposition.

Lesley gave him a disgusted look. 'The meeting would bore you. And what would you do in Portland all that time?'

'I'd find something. Are you leaving now?'

'I'm putting together supper for you, Harry and the kids.'

'Not me,' he corrected. 'I'll be ready to go when you are.'

He was, and he insisted on driving. 'I want to,' he said again, in exactly the same tone that he had used earlier. And Lesley, figuring that she had best save her weapons for big battles that mattered, handed him the keys. If he drove, she could go over her notes for her speech for at least part of the trip, she decided. And when she finished with that she could sleep, or at least pretend to.

So she tried. But Matt was inclined to talk.

'When did you get involved in the school nurse bit?' he wanted to know when she looked up from her notes.

'When I came back last year.'

'Like it?'

'Mm-hmm.'

'It's a good job for you to have with the kids.'

'Yes.'

He paused for a moment, keeping his eyes on the curving road. Then he glanced over at her. 'They're great kids, Les.'

Lesley felt the familiar pangs of worry creep into her heart. 'I think so.'

'I'm glad we've got 'em,' he said quietly.

Her first impulse was to deny that they had anything together. She didn't because she didn't want another fight. She was already weary from a long day at work. She had a speech to give tonight. She didn't need to get worked up over something else at this point. So she deliberately looked away out of the window and didn't say a word.

They stopped for a quick clam supper at a small roadside restaurant just north of Portland, and then Matt dropped her off at her meeting just before seven-thirty.

'What are you going to do?' she asked.

'Listen to you?' he suggested hopefully.

'No way.'

Smiling, he shrugged. 'Walk around, then. Window shop at the mall. Don't worry about it, I'll be here by nine.'

It was past nine and raining by the time the meeting closed. Mary Potter, the regional president, followed her, clucking about the lengthy drive Lesley had ahead of her and advising her to drive carefully and hurry at the same time.

'Don't worry,' said Matt, coming up to them both and taking Lesley's arm. 'I'll see that she gets home.'

Mary Potter looked at him, a startled expression on her usually placid face. Lesley waited for Matt to announce that he was her husband or to do something else equally assertive and equally obnoxious, but he didn't. He simply smiled at Mary and helped Lesley with her jacket. It was Lesley herself who told Mary grudgingly, 'This is my . . . husband, Matt.'

Beaming, Mary clasped his hand. 'I'm so glad you're back safe,' she told him. 'I know how worried Lesley was. Really, it must have been dreadful!'

Matt looked at Lesley curiously. 'Yes, it was.'

'Well, we really ought to be going,' Lesley said hastily. 'It's a long drive.'

'Of course.' Mary shooed them on their way. 'I'll see you at the end of the month in Boston.'

'Were you lurking out here?' Lesley asked Matt the moment they were alone.

'Waiting. *Were* you worried?' he asked, referring to Mary's comment.

'Of course I was,' Lesley said irritably as she clambered into the car.

'I'd never have guessed,' he said drily.

'Well, I was.' Lesley hugged her jacket around her as Matt started up the car and headed out of the car park towards the street.

He paused just before he got there. 'I'm glad,' he said quietly, then pulled out into the street.

They didn't speak again for quite a while. The soft swish of the windscreen wipers was hypnotic, and despite her tenseness whenever she was with him Lesley found his lack of belligerence calming tonight. She was almost lulled into a state of lassitude, when he asked, 'Was that the speech you're giving in Boston?'

She sat up straight. 'Did you hear it?'

'No. You'd finished the speech by the time I got there. More's the pity.'

Lesley didn't agree. 'You wouldn't be interested.'

'Nonsense. I'd like to have heard you. You're really involved, aren't you?'

'Kids matter,' Lesley said simply. 'They're the future of the world.'

Matt didn't reply to that. She looked over to find him staring straight ahead, concentrating on the watery world on the other side of the windscreen. She waited, but in vain. He didn't say a word.

For a brief moment Lesley was disappointed that the conversation had ended, then she told herself she shouldn't be. If he'd agreed with her she would be in more of a dilemma than ever.

Matt maintained his silence for most of the drive, only answering in monosyllables when Lesley asked a question, and declining her offer to drive.

'Are you sure?' she persisted. 'You drove down, and you look tired.'

He looked terrible, as usual, but she wasn't saying that.

'I'm OK,' he brushed her off gruffly. 'Wide awake.' He gave a bitter laugh. 'As always.'

'You get up every night, don't you?' Lesley had got used to seeing the light on downstairs whenever she awakened in the middle of the night.

Matt shrugged.

'Normally I wouldn't even suggest it, but under the circumstances, what about a sedative? I'm sure Dr Payson would——'

'No.'

'But——'

'I said *no*! I don't need drugs. Not that on top of everything else.'

Lesley slanted him a concerned glance. His jaw was tight, his hands clenched on the steering-wheel. 'On top of what else, Matt?' she asked him quietly.

He turned and stared at her. 'You can ask that?' he demanded. 'How about the fact that my marriage is a joke? That my wife's engaged to another man? Not the sort of thing to make a guy sleep well at night, is it?'

So much for concern. 'Damn it, Matt, leave Jacques out of this! You know he's not——'

'Don't tell me he's not part of it! He damned well is. Why, Les? Why, for pity's sake?'

She couldn't answer that.

Matt shook his head. 'Ah, hell. Just go to sleep, Lesley, and leave me alone. You're the one who's done all the work. You're the one who should be tired, not me.'

Torn, Lesley leaned back against the seat and watched him from beneath her lashes. She knew what he wanted, but she wasn't brave enough to say it. And she knew there was more to his not sleeping than how he felt about her and Jacques too. If she wasn't brave enough to tell him she loved him, there were things he didn't seem brave enough to face either.

She pretended to sleep, but she only closed her eyes. She wondered what was going on inside his head, what he was feeling, what he thought, what had happened to him that he wouldn't talk about.

As usual, he didn't give much away. He only sighed a couple of times as he drove staunchly and steadily all the way home.

She must have dozed off, albeit briefly, just before they approached Day's Harbor, for one minute she was watching him concentrate on the road, and the next she felt him shaking her gently and heard him say, 'We're home.'

She blinked and sat up, drawing back as his nearness overwhelmed her. 'So we are.'

She opened the door and got out quickly before the feel of his hands on her excited a response she feared. The rain had eased off a bit, but it gave her an excuse to hurry to the house.

Matt came after her more slowly, and was just coming in at the door as she finished hanging her raincoat on the hook. His brief angry flare-up seemed to have been a thing of the past. There was a quiet, hooded look about him now.

'Thank you for driving,' said Lesley. 'I appreciated it.'

'No problem,' he said politely. He pulled off his jacket and shook his head, sprinkling her with droplets of water.

Lesley went into the kitchen, debated marching straight up the stairs, but couldn't without speaking her mind.

'You really should try to sleep, Matt.'

He scowled. 'Tell Jacques to take a flying leap.'

She lifted her eyebrows. 'And then you'll sleep?'

He shrugged irritably. 'Maybe.'

'And maybe not. Maybe it's more than that.'

He turned away and reached for the evening paper, clearly dismissing her and her insinuations.

But Lesley wasn't going to be deterred. 'How about a glass of warm milk?'

He grimaced. 'Maternal of you.'

Lesley ignored that, not feeling particularly maternal. 'It might help. Well?'

'If you insist.'

She made him a cup, moving about the kitchen quietly so as not to awaken Harry or the children. Matt sat at the kitchen table and watched her, and when she set the mug of steamy milk in front of him he looked at it a moment, then up at her. He smiled slightly—a smile both bitter and wistful. 'Thanks.'

'You're welcome.' She turned towards the stairs. 'It's almost midnight. I'm going up. If you go to bed as soon as you finish that and don't get up until nine, you'll have a good night's sleep.'

'Yeah.'

She gave him an encouraging grin, then hurried up the stairs. She wasn't proof against a smile like his, and she knew she had to put some distance between them while she still had some common sense left.

She took her time getting on her nightgown and getting ready for bed, all the while waiting expectantly for Matt's tread on the stairs. When she didn't hear it, she tiptoed back down.

He was still sitting at the table, his head resting on his arms, the empty mug of milk beside them.

'Matt?'

He lifted his head and looked at her, his hair tousled, his eyes shadowed, his face grim.

'Bed?' she suggested.

'With you?' he asked, faint, but for once not hostile, mockery in his tone.

Lesley shook her head. 'No.'

Their eyes met in a speaking glance. Then he made a face and sighed fatalistically. 'In Teddy's room?'

Lesley nodded hopefully.

He sighed and hauled himself out of his chair, put the empty mug in the sink and followed her up the steps.

'The milk will help,' she assured him when he paused outside Teddy's door.

He shrugged. 'You think so, do you?'

But before she could answer he wrapped her in his arms and kissed her hard, his lips demanding, needing. Then abruptly he let her go. 'There,' he said. 'I reckon that'll help a damned sight more.'

'Ma!'

Lesley tugged the pillow over her head.

'Ma! Mama! Wake up!'

A hand grabbed her shoulder, shook it. She shook it off.

'Ma! Come on—*ven conmigo*! Mama!'

The dream was just getting good, and Lesley didn't want to give it up. Too often she'd had it lately—a dream of herself and Matthew, caressing, loving—and then she'd jerked awake herself, alone and trembling, worse off than she had been before. But this time she had got further and——

'Ma!'

She jerked upright and found Teddy shaking her.

'What is it? Are you dreaming again?' When she'd first brought him and Rita back to the States they both had nightmares. Recently, though, they had stopped.

'Not me—Matt. Come on. Now.' Teddy tugged her arm again and, fully awake at last, Lesley scrambled out of bed to follow him. 'Listen!'

She heard what he meant at once. Matt was moaning, sobbing almost, and the bedsprings creaked as he tossed and turned. She hurried down the hall after Teddy, and into the room he shared with Matt.

'No,' he muttered. 'No!' Louder.

Lesley hurried to him, reaching for him as he thrashed on the mattress, the blanket tangling around his hips. 'Matt.' She spoke calmly, quietly, trying not to betray a flicker of the apprehension she felt. 'Matt. It's all right.'

He jerked away from her, unhearing.

'Matt!'

She had slept beside him whenever he was home for the two years they had stayed together, and she had never, ever seen him like this.

Sometimes, when he'd come home from a particularly long and gruelling overseas assignment, he hadn't been able to unwind right away. Then, regardless of the hour he had got in, he would lie awake, staring at the ceiling, until she came to bed and held him in her arms.

'You can't,' he said hoarsely. 'No! It's too risky.' His voice was urgent. His face contorted. 'No!'

'Matt.' She took him by the shoulders, trying to hold him, but he twisted away from her. 'It's OK, you're free now. You're safe.'

Those words must have penetrated, because he shook his head wildly. 'Free? Never free. Oh, no!' Silent tears seeped out of the corners of his eyes and slid down his cheeks.

'What's wrong with him?' demanded Teddy.

'He's just dreaming.' Lesley was torn, hearing the boy's concern, knowing she should assuage it at the same time as she knew she couldn't let go of the man who was twisting in her arms. 'You did too—remember?'

'Yeah,' Teddy murmured. 'But I never yelled. I never talked. I——'

'You did,' Lesley said. 'You just don't remember. And Matt probably won't remember this. Here.' This last was to Matt whom she was trying to tug to a sitting position. 'Come on, it's OK now,' she soothed.

'No!' He shuddered.

She wrapped her arms around him. Oh lord, what was she doing? 'M-Matt?' Her voice trembled now. Her limbs shook.

His damp head pressed against her shoulder, and she felt him sigh raggedly. His chest heaved, and slowly the random wildness of his nightmare stopped. He drew his head back slightly, lifting it to look at her.

In the darkness, she couldn't tell what he was seeing. He said her name, 'Lesley,' on the barest breath of air, then briefly struggled to pull back, but when her hold on him didn't loosen he sagged once more against her.

She stroked his thick, tousled hair with one hand, kneaded the tense muscles in his neck with the other, and stared into Teddy's wide, worried eyes.

'Don't worry,' she told her son. 'It'll be all right.'

'But——'

'Get back to bed.'

Reluctantly he crossed the room and crawled into his own bed, his eyes never leaving Lesley, who still held Matt in her arms.

Gradually, as his breathing evened, she eased up on her rhythmic kneading and began to draw away. She heard Matt draw an unsteady breath.

'OK now?' she asked softly.

He shook his head.

She brushed a hand through his hair, then stroked his back. 'Do you remember what you were dreaming?'

He swallowed convulsively. For a moment she thought he wasn't going to answer, then, 'Yes.' The word was no more than a whisper.

'Can you talk about——?'

'No!' He stiffened, pulling away from her.

She laid a hand alongside his cheek. 'Never mind, then. It's all right.'

His eyelids drooped and he shook his head wearily.

'Can you go back to sleep now?'

Another shake of the head. He moved to get out of the bed.

'Where are you going?'

'Downstairs.'

'You need to sleep.'

'I can't sleep.' He laughed hoarsely. 'We've already seen what happens when I sleep.'

'But other nights? You must have come up other nights.' She had seen the light, of course. But she hadn't thought he never slept.

'For half an hour or so. Then I went back down.'

'You haven't slept at all?'

'Damned little. When I do—well, you saw what happens.' He swung his legs around and started to stand.

Lesley watched him, torn. But what protest could she make?

'All right.' She paused long enough to give Teddy a kiss. 'Don't worry,' she reassured the boy, 'he'll be fine.'

'I will be,' Matt agreed over his shoulder. 'I just don't want to disturb you again.'

'You won't,' Teddy protested quickly. 'Really. You can stay here.'

'No.' Matt pulled on a pair of jeans and reached for his shirt. Then he gave Teddy a wan smile and padded down the stairs while Lesley hovered at the top, staring after him.

'Shall I . . . come with you?' she ventured.

He didn't even turn around. 'No.'

He walked straight across the living-room, and she heard the door shut to the porch behind him, leaving him alone.

No, she corrected, not quite alone. He had his demons with him.

'Oh, Matt.'

Lesley went back to bed, but she didn't sleep. Her eyes were wide open as she stared at the cracks in the sloping ceiling and her mind saw once more Matt's tears and tortured face.

She had been right about one thing—there was more to his insomnia than her relationship with Jacques. Jacques had had nothing to do with this at all.

But then, what had he dreamed? What had been too risky? Who had he been speaking to when he'd said no?

She rolled over and stared out at the moon that hung just above the pine trees at the far side of the yard. Then she rolled back and stared at the narrow sliver of light that shone still beneath her bedroom door. She looked at the clock. 2:19. She looked at the ceiling. 2:38. At the door. 2:57. At the moon. 3:12. At the trees. 3:28.

She waited for footsteps, for a sign that Matt had tired out and was ready to come up and try to sleep again.

None came.

None came up the stairs, at least. Faintly she could hear movement down below. The occasional creak of a floorboard, the closing of a window, the swish of a door. Silence. Then a while later the floorboards again.

He might be getting well as far as his wound went, but he was going to make himself sick doing this. So he didn't like sedatives. Neither did she. But he had to do something to get the sleep he required.

Only one thing had got him to sleep in the past when he had lain awake, his mind spinning with the sight of events he'd reported on. Only one thing had taken the edge off his anxiety and given him much needed rest.

She knew how to help him, all right. The question was—did she dare?

*   *   *

'What are you doing?' Matt spun around at the sound of her footsteps and the creak of the door to the porch.

Lesley didn't answer, just went to him and took him by the hand. It had taken her another half-hour to muster the courage to do this. She wasn't about to make it subject for discussion. 'You do need to sleep.'

'I told you—*I can't!*'

'I'll help you.' Tugging his hand, she led him back through the living-room.

'Not more hot milk,' he told her gruffly.

'Obviously not.' Her voice was dry. She flicked off the light and drew him with her up the stairs.

'I can't go in there,' he said as they approached Teddy's room. 'I'll wake——'

'Not his room.' And Lesley led him into her own.

'Sex?' He sounded incredulous as he yanked her to a halt and stared at her in the darkened room.

For a moment her composure slipped, and she glowered at him. 'Don't be an ass, Matthew.'

'Well, what the hell else——'

She pointed at the bed. 'Get in and lie down.'

'But——''

'In,' she commanded.

If he didn't obey in a minute she was going to turn and run herself. It was taking every ounce of will-power and not one shred of common sense for her to do this. It could very well destroy her. And he wanted to argue about it!

Just when she thought she would be the one to crack, the one to shrug her shoulders and say, 'Oh, well, if you'd rather pace the floor . . .' Matt nodded jerkily and began to unbutton his shirt.

He tossed it on to her dresser. His hands went to the button of his jeans. He paused, looking at her, but when she bit her tongue against objecting, he undid the fastener, lowered the zip, and let them slide down his legs. A soft thud and clank told her that they, along with his wallet and change, had hit the floor. He didn't remove his briefs, thank heavens, but got into the bed still wearing them, stretching out cautiously beneath the sheet and folding his arms under his head.

'Now what?' he asked curiously, his voice betraying the slightest tremor.

Lesley mustered every molecule of matter-of-factness she could summon. 'Now this,' she said, tossed her own robe aside, and slid in beside him.

Who got the bigger shock, she didn't know.

All the mental gymnastics and preparation in the world hadn't prepared her for the solid warmth of Matthew's body hard against her own. And for an instant Matthew stiffened so completely, she nearly thought rigor mortis had set in. But she could hardly back out now.

So, mustering her courage, she snuggled her body next to his, looping one arm over him to hug him across the chest.

His heart was slamming—she could feel it. He seemed barely to be breathing. She felt that too.

'Lesley?' His voice was no more than a croak.

'Mmm?' She lifted her head and looked down at him. The little she could see of his expression in the moonlight betrayed apprehension, tension—all the things she was trying to assuage.

'This is supposed to help?' His laugh was rough and threaded with despair.

'It used to,' she reminded him. 'Remember?'

He sighed raggedly. 'Oh, hell! I don't want memories, Lesley.'

'Then forget them. Forget everything.'

'I can't forget,' he said angrily, trying to turn away from her. 'That's the whole problem.'

Her arm tightened around him, drawing him closer, pulling him back, bringing his bare chest snug against the flimsy gown covering her own. He resisted for a moment, tensing further. But Lesley wouldn't give in. OK, then, we'll lie here and remember together.'

'No,' he muttered. But he didn't pull away. He didn't move a muscle, just lay fast against her, letting her hold him, letting her stroke his back softly and rhythmically. The clock downstairs chimed three-forty-five. An owl hooted. A very tentative morning bird-call sounded across the way. Time moved on, but Lesley didn't. And gradually she felt the tension in him ease.

She moved over on to her back, and Matt moved with her. His head lay heavily against her breasts, his hand, which had been clenched, relaxed, the fingers splayed on her thigh. His breathing, which had been shallow, deepened and slowed. He nuzzled against her breast, then sighed.

'Matthew?' Lesley whispered against the top of his dark head.

She got no response.

Her hands slid down the strong curve of his spine and clasped together at the small of his back. It had been like this after Beirut, after Johannesburg, after El Salvador and Belfast. And each time he had left her.

Was she a fool to let it happen again?

CHAPTER SEVEN

THERE were lumps in the porridge, Teddy couldn't find his favourite fishing sinker, and Rita left her bed unmade. In other words, Lesley told herself, it was a morning exactly like any other.

But it wasn't—because she had awakened in Matt Colter's arms.

It had just gone six when she'd opened her eyes to the sight of the top of Matt's tousled dark head. But once she had seen it, once she had remembered where she was, she couldn't close them again.

She couldn't anyway, of course. She had to get up and go to work. But it wasn't the thought of work that kept her awake and aware of him. She lay there absorbing the sensations, breathing in the warm male scent of him, letting her hands learn the feel of his skin again, and her body the welcome weight of his.

Was it indeed welcome? she asked herself.

A very good question.

Her body thought so, there was no doubt about that. But her mind was sceptical.

And her emotions? Her emotions were, frankly, at war with one another. One part of her wanted him desperately, just as much as she always had. And the other shrank from risking further pain, shrank from caring again, from becoming the woman her mother had become.

At least Matt had slept, she told herself. And that was really the purpose of the exercise. That *was* all she had intended, wasn't it?

She didn't wait to hear the end of that particular internal

conversation. Instead she slid slowly and carefully out from beneath him, easing him on to the mattress. His hand clutched hers for a moment, hanging on tightly. But there wasn't the anxiety in him now, and when she prised his fingers loose he resisted only a moment before sighing and letting her go.

She slipped off the bed and picked up her robe, sliding her arms into it and tying the sash. She started for the door, then stopped and turned back.

It was too tempting, and goodness knew when she would get an opportunity like this again. Goodness knew when—if ever—she would be able to drink in the sight of him again, love him again, with impunity. So, for as long as she dared, she stood quite still and simply looked at him. Then she turned away and closed the door of the room behind her before the temptation grew and she found herself crawling back into the bed.

Matt didn't awaken before she left for school, and she was glad of that. She didn't know what to say to him—or, worse, what he would say to her—and she didn't want to find out in front of the children.

Once she got to school, she put him out of her mind for the rest of the day. It wasn't easy, but it was necessary. And fortunately there were enough bumps, scrapes and other disasters to keep her mind fairly fully occupied until she left for home.

But on the way her turmoil grew. Heaven only knew what he thought she'd meant by last night, but, if heaven knew, Lesley had a pretty good guess. And it wasn't what she had meant. She needed to disabuse him at once of whatever erroneous notions he might have picked up. Unfortunately he was out.

'Went clamming, him and Ted,' Uncle Harry told her. 'Said they'd bring enough for supper. Suit you?'

'Fine,' Lesley mumbled.

Uncle Harry folded the paper back to do the crossword. 'Workin' hard, he is. Settlin' in.'

Lesley grunted a reply, not sure what he wanted to hear, not sure what she felt.

'Says he likes it, too.'

'Writing for a local weekly?' Lesley couldn't disguise her disbelief.

'Does his own work in the morning—a book on his hot-shot days. Does articles for me in the afternoons until the kids come home. Balance, he says,' Uncle Harry reported.

'Balance?' It wasn't a word she would have expected of Matt Colter.

'Balance,' Harry concurred. 'Seems to be workin', too,' he added. 'Looks a damned sight better today than he did. Y'ought t'try it yourself, 'stead of workin' so hard all the time. We hardly see you any more.'

The injustice of that remark made Lesley bristle, but she didn't reply. She held her tongue and waited to talk to Matt.

When he and Teddy got back, however, there was still no opportunity to speak to him. The very idea of discussing in front of the children and over a bucket of clams just why she had taken him into her bed last night didn't even bear thinking about.

Matt didn't ask, either. But she felt his eyes on her all evening, following her every move with an expression both wistful and tender. It made her positively shiver.

He looked better, she thought. More rested, less tense. But she didn't dare comment on it, instead busying herself with melting the butter and setting out large cloth napkins on the dining-room table. He came upon her once when she was alone, but it wasn't long enough to say her piece, and he didn't give her a chance to anyway, forestalling any words on her part by softly saying, 'Thanks.'

Lesley felt colour rise in her cheeks as she ducked her

head and murmured, 'You're welcome.' Then she darted out to the dining-room with the drawn butter for the clams. Then, because she wanted to be sure he didn't read anything more into it than she meant, she tossed out, 'I hope you'll sleep better from now on.'

'Oh, I'm sure I shall,' he replied, smiling.

Four hours later, when she went upstairs to retire, she found out why.

He was lying in her bed.

She stopped stock still in the doorway, her jaw dropping. 'Matthew!'

He gave her a slow, seductive smile.

Abruptly she closed her mouth and shut the door behind her so Uncle Harry, who was still puttering around in his room, couldn't hear.

'What do you think you're doing here?' she began, outraged.

'Waiting for you.'

He was shirtless, and very probably less all the rest of his clothes too, she thought, judging from past experience. He lay with his arms folded behind his head, the sheet hitting him mid-chest. Lesley remembered his waiting for her just like that during the early days of their marriage. He would have already showered and, when she came out of the bath, she would find him lying there, waiting, his hair damp, his dark eyes lambent with desire as he watched her shed her robe and come to bed.

She shook her head, deliberately clearing it of all such reminiscences. 'No, Matt.'

'Yes, Lesley.'

'I don't want to sleep with you.'

He sat up. 'I don't believe you.'

'I don't.' She was hugging her arms across her chest, her back hard against the door.

He flung back the blanket and swung his long legs out of

the bed. She was right; he was every bit as naked as she'd feared he would be, but somehow the foreknowledge didn't prepare her. She squeezed her eyes shut.

But she didn't need eyes to tell her when he'd come to stand right in front of her. She could feel the heat of his body, hear the sound of his breathing even as she willed him to go away.

Then he touched her. She drew back.

'Lesley.' His voice was softly insistent. 'Come to bed.'

'No.' Her heart was thundering.

His hands came to her waist, then started to draw her sweater up over her breasts. She hugged her arms more tightly against herself.

He chuckled. 'Come on, Les.' He bent forward, touching his lips to her jawline, drawing them lightly along it. She shivered, and Matt groaned.

'Les.' He whispered her name into her ear, then nibbled it.

It was torture, resisting. Wanting and yet fearing. Lesley stiffened and willed her body to deny him, to deny herself. But her body was no fool. It recognised immediately the longed-for touch. It welcomed at once the familiar lips, the light stroking of his hands along her ribs, the gentle brush of his eyelashes against her cheek and the rough scrape of his cheek against her jaw.

He reached behind her, flipping the light switch, plunging the room into darkness. Lesley opened her mouth to protest and found it covered by his lips.

They hadn't kissed like this since Matt had come back. In fact, they had never kissed like this before. Dams broke, storms raged, a flood of pent-up feelings Lesley couldn't have put a name to welled up in her, swamped her, carrying her away just as Matt was doing now as he brought her to the bed and laid her down upon it, never taking his lips from hers.

He was beside her in an instant, his hands trembling as they stroked the sweater over her head. 'I missed you,' he muttered, recapturing her lips with his own. His tongue sought hers and, with a groan, she gave him what he wanted to find. For there was no use pretending now. No use fighting it. She wanted it—wanted him—every bit as much as he wanted her.

Her arms went around him, holding him to her, and her lips travelled along his jawline, then down his neck, then traced his collarbone as she nuzzled against the whorls of hair on his chest. The scent of him intoxicated her. A mixture of pure male, sandalwood, and something indefinably Matt seduced her, robbed her of her reason, freed her for an experience more profound, more moving than all the common sense and good intentions she had been mustering for days.

With trembling fingers she learned him again, outlining his shoulders, then drawing firm lines down his back, moulding the rise and curve of his spine and the firm flesh of his buttocks. He groaned and pulled away from her, rising to his knees and settling himself between her legs.

'Ah, Les!' He seemed unable to stop touching her. His hands caressed her arms, her breasts, her ribs, her belly. In the silver glow of moonlight she saw his face taut with passion as he smiled down at her.

'I need you so much,' he muttered, ducking his head. And then his body covered her, and, shaking, he sought the safety of her, gave himself up to her, and let her guide him home.

Lesley's hands locked against the small of his back, holding him securely, feeling him trembling against her, trembling herself, revelling in the storm that built within them. Then she loosed her hands a fraction, and he began to move. The storm broke over them, casting them up, blowing them away. And they only had each other to cling to until at last they drifted down to earth again.

She couldn't regret it. Not yet.

Tomorrow, perhaps. Even an hour from now. Whenever reason reasserted itself, when common sense and memories of past experience held sway.

But for now she could only feel peace, contentment, a sense of having travelled long and lonely trails until at last she had come home.

The weight of Matt's body lulled her, the receding thunder of his heart soothed her, and the wetness of his cheek against hers——

She jerked, her fingers coming up to touch his face. 'Matt? Are you crying?'

'Of course not.' He sounded offended, gruff.

But her hand came away wet. She touched it to her lips; it tasted of salt.

'Oh, Matt,' she murmured. 'Oh, Matt!' And she wrapped him in her arms and held him close.

Matt sighed, wiped a forearm across his eyes, and rested his head against her breasts. 'I love you,' he muttered. And then he was asleep.

Saturdays, for longer than Lesley wanted to remember, had been nothing special. Another long day—a little housework, a few charts, a chance to read the newspaper, play with the kids, put her feet up for a few moments in between times.

This Saturday was different.

It felt different from the moment she felt the first glimmerings of consciousness. Somehow she was warmer, cosier, more content. And when she opened her eyes she knew why.

She was looking straight into Matt's.

He was raised up on one elbow, one hand propping his dark, shaggy head while he looked down on her. He was smiling, though his brown eyes were serious as they met hers. 'Good morning,' he said softly, and leaned down to touch his lips lightly to her nose.

'Good morning.' Lesley's voice was husky with sleep, wobbly with apprehension. The worries she had abandoned last night were already swarming back. She tried to ease her way back on to the pillows, warm, cosy contentment fleeing in the face of the morning sun.

'You'd better tell Jacques,' Matt said gravely.

Jacques! Lesley shut her eyes, groaning. 'Tell him what?' she croaked. 'That I slept with you?'

A grin crooked the corner of Matt's mouth. 'Well, as much as I'd like you to, I think it might be tactless. Why don't you just say you've had second thoughts?'

'I'm having second thoughts. About you,' Lesley protested, pushing herself away from him, but he just edged closer. His bare thigh insinuated itself between hers beneath the covers.

'About him,' Matt corrected. 'I'll take care of the ones you're having about me.'

'But——'

He silenced her with a kiss. 'You can't mean to marry him now,' he said, his expression worried. 'Can you?'

Of course she couldn't. She should never have said yes to him in the first place, should never have even considered it. But safety first had seemed the only way to go then. Rejected by the man she had never stopped loving, she'd had to decide who she would settle for instead. She shook her head, suddenly ashamed.

Matt breathed a sigh of relief. His fingers tangled in her hair, stroking it away from her face, then brushing her cheekbones with his thumbs. 'Thank heaven,' he murmured.

Lesley stiffened.

'What's wrong?' he demanded.

'I can't . . . I don't . . .'

'Can't what? Don't what?' He looked down at her intently.

She drew an unsteady breath. 'You're right,' she said after a moment of thought gathering. 'I can't . . . marry Jacques, but . . .'

He waited, his contentment gone. 'But what?' he ground out.

'But this . . . what we did . . .'

'Made love,' he said flatly.

Lesley nodded jerkily. 'I . . . don't know . . . I can't . . .'

'Can't what, for pity's sake?' he demanded. 'Don't tell me you didn't want to, Lesley! I won't believe you.'

'I . . . did . . . want to. Then. But now . . .' Her voice trailed off again.

'You still do,' he insisted. 'Want me to prove it?' He levered himself up further, his free hand going to her bare breast, caressing it, smoothing the silky soft flesh as he brought it to a peak.

Lesley lifted her hand to still his, and their fingers locked, then lowered to rest between their bodies. The warm strength of his hand enveloping hers made her remember how she had enveloped him. And then he was kissing her again, and she was lost again as he set about proving exactly what he said he would prove.

'Told you so,' he whispered softly in her ear as they lay together afterwards, replete and exhausted.

And he had, of course. But that didn't solve her problem. She sighed and shut her eyes, but before she could think of any way to say what she feared there was a brief tap on the door and it was flung open.

'Mama,' Rita began, 'd'you know where Dad——' She stopped and stared at her mother and the man who lay beside her under the covers. 'Oh!' she said. 'He's here, Teddy!' she shouted, and banged the door shut again. 'He's here!' And Lesley heard her footsteps scampering down the hall.

Her cheeks burned. 'Swell,' she muttered.

'It was. Swell, that is,' said Matt, grinning.

'I don't mean that,' Lesley said crossly, 'and you know it. I mean Rita seeing you here.'

'What's wrong with it? We're married. You should have been worried about them seeing me spending the night in Teddy's room instead.'

'They expected that.'

'I didn't,' he said drily.

'Well, you should have. Besides, they knew we were separated. And now . . .' She stopped.

'Now what?'

'Now they'll think we aren't.'

'We aren't.'

She looked at him, disbelieving.

He understood the look. 'We aren't,' he repeated forcefully. 'We're married and we're going to stay that way.'

'Not if you go off again the way you——'

'I told you, I'm not going anywhere. Home and hearth, that's me, kiddo.'

Lesley shook her head wearily. 'I wish I could believe that.'

'You can believe it,' he insisted.

But words didn't make it so. She remembered that all too well. Her own father had said the same words time and time again. 'I'm home to stay, Madge,' he would tell her mother.

But it never lasted. 'He's just got itchy feet,' Lesley's mother would excuse him.

But, whatever he had, life in Bangor, where Lesley had grown up, was never enough for him. He would be home for two weeks or months or, once, even for two years, and then, without warning, he would be gone again, leaving Lesley and her mother to pick up the pieces of their lives.

Lesley did. She was young and resilient. But Jack Fuller's peripatetic nature took a toll on his wife. Over the years she had turned from a smiling, confident young girl to a hurt, weary, distrustful woman. A woman Lesley would not want to resemble.

The question was, of course, would Matt be like her father?

He said not. So far he had lived up to what he said. But was he really trustworthy? Or was he merely marking time with them until some great earth-shaking event came along that interested him more?

She didn't say any of this to Matt, however. What would be the point? He would argue. He would say he wasn't her father. But words couldn't make her believe that he wouldn't do what her father had. He couldn't make her believe with mere words that her life wasn't going to come apart at the seams the same way her mother's had again and again.

Proving to her that she loved him and wanted him was no difficult task. He had done it, and he had done it well. But proving that she could trust him, that he really had changed his tune, would take a little longer.

'We'll see,' she said. She eased back the covers and slid out of bed, feeling self-conscious of her nakedness in the morning sunlight. She reached for underwear, a pair of jeans and a T-shirt and hastily slipped them on. Once dressed, she could look at Matt again. He was still lying in the bed, his eyes following her every move, his expression serious.

'I mean it, Les,' he said. 'Believe me.'

She nodded—it was the best she could do—then pressed her lips together. 'I'll be making pancakes if the kids haven't already eaten. Do you want some?'

A corner of his mouth lifted. 'Sounds good. I'll shower and be right down.'

Lesley could hear the children's chatter as she went down the stairs. But the moment she walked into the kitchen the conversation ceased. The two of them stared at her, eyes wide and hopeful.

Feeling her cheeks burn, Lesley made to bustle past them, starting to say something about the pancakes, but Teddy spoke up before she had opened her mouth.

'So it's all right now?' he asked.

'All right?' Lesley ducked her head to peer into the refrigerator, playing dumb.

'You're sleeping with him.'

'Teddy!' She glared at him, then shot a glance at his little sister.

'She tol' me,' he defended himself stoutly. 'I just meant, he is staying, isn't he?'

'He says so.'

'Don't you believe him?'

Lesley pulled out a carton of eggs and sighed. 'I don't know what to believe.'

'Well, I believe him,' said Teddy, then added with childish logic, 'Why should he want to go? Everything he wants in the whole world is right here.'

Did he tell you that? Lesley wanted to ask. But she didn't. Instead, she just said, 'How about some pancakes for breakfast?' And her suggestion diffused further speculation.

She made blueberry ones with the last of the berries she had frozen from the previous summer, glad that she had managed to make them last until almost picking-time again. She was just putting them on the platter when Matt came into the kitchen.

His hair was still damp from the shower, and he wore a pair of low-slung faded denim jeans and a forest-green polo shirt. He looked disgustingly well-rested and extraordinarily handsome. Obviously making love to her agreed with him. And, if Lesley was still in turmoil, Matt clearly wasn't.

He tousled Teddy's hair, gave Rita's pigtail a fond tug, and bestowed on Lesley a smile so filled with tenderness that her heart danced a polka in her chest. Quickly she turned away and ferreted the syrup bottles out of the cupboard.

'Good morning,' he said to no one in particular, but quite suddenly Lesley sensed his presence behind her, and before she knew it felt the touch of his lips on the nape of her neck.

'Sleep well?' Uncle Harry boomed as he came in through the back door, shedding his jacket.

'Indeed we did,' murmured Matt, and Lesley went bright red.

'Me too,' Harry went on, oblivious. 'Gorgeous day out. I walked to the point. The rest of you are a pack of bums.'

'Not me,' Rita protested. 'I was watching cartoons.'

'Kids' stuff!' Teddy snorted.

'You watched 'em too,' Rita maintained. 'Only Mama didn't. And Matt,' she added as she looked at them both from beneath dark lashes, then caught Teddy's eye and giggled.

Uncle Harry looked at the children, nonplussed. Then his gaze shifted to Matt and Lesley. A smile slowly dawned on his face. 'Ah!'

Lesley could almost hear his sigh of relief. He crossed the room and gave her a gentle peck on the cheek. 'I'm so glad.'

Lesley managed a smile. She didn't have the same confidence everyone else seemed to, but for now she allowed herself to be swept along by theirs. She was tired of fighting her own heart.

Maybe she could learn to believe, try to trust. Really, what other choice did she have?

'D'you want to come with us to set the rocket off, Mama?' Teddy asked her as he finished his breakfast, and she looked up to find she was the object of all eyes. Considering the fuss she had made about the rocket a few days ago, she shouldn't be surprised.

'Well, I——' The habit of avoiding Matt was so ingrained now that she almost refused without thinking. But then she thought, why not? It was a family sort of thing to do. Hadn't she often dreamed of living in the sort of family where parents and children played in the park together on a Saturday? Maybe if she went along with it, maybe if she acted as if she believed, her fondest dream would actually come true. She smiled. 'Yes, all right, I will.'

Teddy whooped his enthusiasm. 'Let's go, then!'

'Not now.' Matt pushed back his chair and carried his dishes to the sink. 'Chores first. And you can help fill the dishwasher for a start.'

Teddy groaned, but only got a stern look for his effort. Lesley felt a faint remnant of annoyance at the way he so easily took direction from Matt. But then she found that she was glad. If Matt was truly going to be the father of these children, it was right that he have their love and respect.

The afternoon proved to her that he'd gone a long way towards gaining it.

Lesley packed a picnic lunch and they went to the park overlooking the Bay. It had broad lawns, playground equipment, climbing rocks, a backdrop of pines, and was the perfect setting for a family outing.

And a family outing was exactly what they had. Matt helped Rita figure out how to swing across a rope apparatus, thereby earning hugs, kisses and everlasting gratitude from his daughter. Then he and Teddy put the finishing touches on the rocket. After lunch, while Lesley pushed Rita on the swings, Teddy and Matt set the rocket up for launching.

Then, while Lesley held her breath and Rita shrieked, Teddy set off the rocket without damaging himself in the least.

'See?' he shouted, running up and flinging his arms around her. 'I told you we could do it! Just like Robby and his dad. I knew it!' He turned and beamed at Matt. 'I'm really glad you're my dad!' And then he took off with the rocket to set it up again.

He didn't even hear Matt's softly spoken, 'And I'm glad you're my son.'

But Lesley heard it, and when Matt took her hand and led her to the swings, seating her in one and lowering himself into the one next to it, she said, 'You've changed your tune, then, haven't you?'

The sun came out from behind a cloud, bathing them both in the warm summer light. They swung gently, side by side, letting the breeze off the ocean lift their hair.

'I mean, weren't you the man who didn't want any children? "None. Not ever."' She quoted an early Matt Colter diatribe.

Matt nodded. He swung back and forth, and Lesley pushed so that she moved in unison with him.

'So what happened?'

For a time he didn't answer. Then he looked out at the children, chasing across the grass, Teddy shouting something to Rita in Spanish which she answered just as promptly in English. 'Family sounds good to me,' he said finally. 'It's something you come to appreciate . . . over there.'

A topic they had certainly skirted around before. A hundred times she had been tempted, then pulled back at his reaction, as if she were probing an open wound he couldn't bear to have touched, which in a way, Lesley supposed, she was.

But now, because things were changing between them, she had to ask more, had to know more, had to try to understand him. 'Did you spend a lot of time . . . thinking about . . . family?'

He gave a rueful laugh and lifted his face to the sun. 'Damn little else. Made me see things I'd never seen before.'

He pushed away again, then came to a halt next to where she sat. 'Opened my eyes. When you're stuck in one place for months at a time, no place to go, nothing to read, no news at all, you think. You think a lot. But you don't spend a lot of time on things you did. You think about all the things you didn't do, the things you *wished* you'd done.

'And what I wished for——' he looked squarely into her eyes '—was you.'

He reached for the chain that held her swing, halting it, then drew her towards him. Then he leaned across the foot of space that separated them and gave her a lingering kiss on the lips, a kiss that told her more vividly than any words just how much he had missed her. She returned it, willing to admit finally how much she had missed him.

Teddy hooted at them, and Matt looked up grinning and shouted, 'Mind your own business!'

To which Teddy shouted back, 'It is my business!'

'I guess it is,' murmured Matt. 'He's part of my family, after all.'

The words made Lesley start to smile. Then he reached for her, pulling her out of her swing and taking her on to his lap. 'But you are the centre of my family, the woman it revolves around. I love you,' he said, wrapping his arms around her and burying his face into the nape of her neck, 'more than anyone or anything else on earth.'

And, at that moment at least, Lesley believed him.

CHAPTER EIGHT

AN hour later she wasn't sure.

They had come back from the park, arms around each other's waist, happy and exhausted, to be met at the door by Uncle Harry.

'I reckon I died and was born again an answering machine,' he complained. 'Phone nearly rung itself off th'hook.'

'What phone calls?' asked Lesley.

'Reporters. Editors. Matt's mother. And Jacques.'

'Oh, lord,' said Matt and Lesley as one.

'What did they want?' asked Matt, scowling.

'Your mother, you. The editors, your reaction.'

'To what?' Matt shrugged off his windbreaker and turned to hang it up.

'They caught a couple of your terrorists.'

Matt's head jerked around. 'Who?'

'Don't know. You could call any of these guys.' Harry handed him the list of phone messages. 'I'm sure they'd be glad to tell you.'

Lesley came to look over Matt's shoulder, but he was already heading for the telephone.

'And you,' Harry said before she could follow Matt, 'Jacques said you're supposed to call 'im no matter when you get back.'

'What did you tell him?' Lesley hoped Harry had more tact than she often gave him credit for.

'Told 'im you were out,' Harry said, then fixed her with a challenging stare. 'You can tell 'im the rest.'

She would have to, of course. At once. As soon as Matt

got off the phone. She could hear him talking in the other room now, asking questions, listening. And when she ventured in she saw him nodding and raking fingers through his hair. It was a posture she remembered. She had seen it countless times before. It meant he was interested, involved, and at any second would be flinging down the phone and heading for the door.

Despite all his assurances, would it begin again? Was this the phone call that would tempt him, that would tantalise him? Was this the story he wouldn't be able to resist? She knew he had had others recently—job offers, stories that Dave Carlisle or other editors had thought he would snap up, exactly the way Griswald had predicted he would. But so far he had declined. He hadn't shown the faintest bit of interest in any of them.

He was interested now.

'Yeah,' she heard him say, 'that's right. Sons of bitches, both of 'em.' Then, 'No . . . no.'

He prowled around the room, picking up an ashtray, scowling at it, setting it down and searching in his pockets for a cigarette. 'No,' he said again. Then, with exaggerated patience, 'Because I don't want to.'

Lesley held her breath, waiting while Matt listened to what the man on the other end of the line said.

'I just . . . don't,' she heard him growl. 'Look, Dave, I mean it.' He paced to the end of the phone cord, then back. 'I know it's a good story—I'd be a fool if I didn't. But I'm not going. I just don't want to do it.' His eyes met Lesley's and he gave her a weary grimace and a shrug.

She gave him a smile in return, rooting for him.

Obviously Dave was still talking, for Matt sighed and did another lap of the front room. Then Lesley heard him say even more forcefully, 'I've just had enough . . .' Another lap of the room. 'Of course I'll let you know if I change my mind. But I won't be changing it.'

He grimaced at whatever Dave Carlisle said, then he added, 'I would appreciate it if you'd keep me posted, though. Thanks. 'Bye,' and dropped the receiver on to the hook.

He had scarcely hung up when the phone rang again.

Picking it up, he said almost at once, 'No, he's not here. Sorry,' and hung up.

'For you?' Lesley guessed.

Matt made a face. 'Harry's right. This could be a zoo.'

But Lesley didn't care if it was or not as long as Matt was still saying no. 'Carlisle wanted you to go over there, didn't he?'

Matt crossed the room and took her in his arms. 'Yes.'

She stiffened. 'I thought so.'

'But you don't see me packing, do you?' he said into her hair.

Lesley shook her head and hugged him, then looked up into his eyes. 'Weren't you tempted, though?'

'Nope. Nothing tempts me these days but you.' His hands tugged her shirt out of the waistband of her jeans.

The phone rang again.

'Cripes,' he muttered. 'What is it?' he barked into the receiver, and Lesley heard Jacques' voice faintly asking,

'May I speak to Lesley?'

'About my wife——' Matt began, but Lesley snatched the receiver out of his hand.

'Oh, hi, Jacques,' she said breathlessly, while Matt nibbled on her ear and rocked his hips against her and tried to take the receiver out of her hand. 'Uncle Harry said you'd called.'

'Where have you been?'

'Out. I—er—went for a walk,' she said lamely, squirming against the sensation of Matt's lips on the sensitive skin of her neck.

'Avoiding Colter?' he guessed. 'You can always come

over to my place.'

'No, thanks. I—I need to talk to you.' She ducked abruptly, stifling a giggle, and wriggled out of Matt's arms to barricade herself behind the couch.

'Let me talk to him,' Matt mouthed.

Lesley shook her head.

'Glad to hear it,' said Jacques, oblivious. 'It's about time.'

'Now,' Lesley said, backing up. Matt was edging around one side of the couch, a teasing grin on his face.

'Even better,' Jacques went on. 'I'll pick you up.'

'I don't know. I——' she began, edging back the opposite way from Matt, trying to find words to prepare Jacques at least a bit for what she would have to tell him.

But before she could say another word she heard, 'Be there in fifteen minutes,' and he hung up. She was standing there with the receiver still hanging from nerveless fingers when Matt climbed over the couch.

'You didn't tell him,' he accused.

'What was I supposed to do, just toss it into the conversation? "Oh, by the way, I don't want to marry you any more?" I will,' she promised quickly when he scowled at her. 'I . . . I'm going out with him.'

'The hell you are!'

'I don't mean "out with" as in a date,' Lesley said hastily in the face of his ferocious frown. 'I mean to talk.'

Matt's lips pressed together in a thin line. His brows drew down. 'What's to talk about?'

Lesley gave him a pained look. 'You know very well.'

'You don't have to go out with him to tell him that.'

'Well, I'm not going to send him a letter.'

'Why not?' he asked stubbornly.

'Because I'm not. I have more feeling for him than that. And you ought to be glad I do. Would you really want a wife who didn't give a hoot about people's feelings, who ran roughshod over them, who was only concerned about herself, about her own life, her own needs and desires?'

Matt went still. 'No,' he mumbled after a moment, 'I wouldn't.'

'Well then?' said Lesley, but he still looked shaken. 'Sorry,' she muttered. 'I should get down from my pulpit, I guess.'

'No. I . . . I understand.' He gave her a thin-lipped, serious smile, and he didn't protest in the slightest when several minutes later Rita bounced in from the kitchen to announce,

'Jacques is here.'

Lesley came into the kitchen to find him waiting. His wavy dark hair was windblown, and he had the collar of his jacket turned up against the evening breeze. He looked dear and handsome and confident as he smiled when Lesley came into the room, and she felt like a total heel.

She felt an even bigger heel when he came over and kissed her gently. She turned quickly, making a production out of plucking her windbreaker off the hook, but Jacques didn't seem to notice her nervousness.

'How about a piece of pie at Kate's?' he suggested as he held the door for her.

'Oh—er—sure.' She was of divided mind, actually. Part of her thought they didn't need an audience for what she was about to tell him. Another part suspected that the distraction of a public place might be her salvation.

Jacques seemed to have no notion of what she was about to say. He wouldn't have been so cheerful if he did. He whistled as he walked her out to his car, and he gave her a grin and a wink as he handed her in.

He drove a Porsche, not standard equipment for most lobstermen. But then, Jacques wasn't your average lobsterman. He had worked himself crazy for the last five years, and he had several boats and a thriving business to show for it.

'What else did I have to do when you left me?' he had asked after Lesley had returned from Colombia with the children and they had tentatively begun dating again.

She closed her eyes now and wished she hadn't been so foolish. It was bad enough that she had rejected him once. She couldn't imagine how to do it a second time. She wished it hadn't worked out the way it had. If only she hadn't just said yes!

Jacques got in on the driver's side, started up the car and spun out down the driveway. 'Alone at last,' he said, and reached for her hand.

Lesley gave him a wan smile.

His eyes narrowed slightly and he turned back to concentrate on his driving. 'So,' he said when they were headed down the road towards town, 'if he hasn't left yet, he must be packing, huh?'

Lesley frowned. 'Why?'

He shot her a curious look. 'Because they caught 'em.'

'Oh, you mean his captors?'

'Yeah. No doubt they'll be calling him, wanting him to go back over there and cover it. It's a natural.'

'They've already called,' Lesley said as Jacques pulled up in front of Kate's Pastry Shop.

'So when's he going?'

'He isn't.'

Jacques stopped the car and stared at her. 'You're joking, right?'

Lesley shook her head and wished for a moment she had taken the coward's way out and let Matt break the news to him, even as she knew she couldn't. 'That's what I need to talk to you about.'

Kate Blackledge's Pastry Shop was crowded as it usually was during the tourist season. There were scarcely any spare tables in the tiny room, and no chairs at all along the narrow counter where most of her regulars sat and gorged themselves on her pies and cakes. But a couple were just leaving a table in front of the bay window, and Jacques commandeered it, silently seating Lesley and then taking the chair opposite her. He leaned his elbows on the table and rested his chin on his fists.

'What's going on?'

Before Lesley could answer, Kate appeared at their table. 'What can I get you?' she asked, smiling down at Jacques.

Jacques looked momentarily irritated. 'You choose,' he said to Lesley.

'Got any fresh rhubarb pie left?'

Kate nodded.

'Two rhubarbs and two coffees,' said Jacques, dismissing her.

Kate nodded, her smile fading a bit as she started to walk away. Then she stopped and said to Lesley, 'I thought . . . isn't your . . . husband still in town?' She looked from Lesley to Jacques and back again curiously. It was no secret that Jacques had been courting her prior to Matt's release. But since Matt had come back he had stayed away. Kate must have wondered how things stood now.

Lesley took a deep breath. 'Yes, he is.'

Kate's gaze flickered to Jacques briefly. 'Is he . . . staying?'

'Yes.'

Jacques frowned.

Kate smiled. 'That's wonderful. I'm really glad for you.' And with one more hungry, lingering glance at Jacques she left to get the pie. Lesley's eyes followed the young woman thoughtfully, curious herself now.

'What do you think of Kate Blackledge?' she asked Jacques.

'I don't think of Kate Blackledge,' he replied stonily.

Lesley sighed. So much for an easy way out.

'What's Colter staying for?' Jacques leaned forward, his

green eyes boring into her with intensity.

'He's going to work with Uncle Harry.'

Jacques snorted. 'On a two-bit weekly? Gimme a break!'

'He's doing some writing on his own.'

'Memoirs? He's only thirty-four—not quite over the hill yet. Two months and he'll be gone,' he wagered.

Lesley laid her hands on the table, fascinated by the way they didn't even tremble when her insides were quivering like mad. 'He says he's staying, Jacques,' she said slowly and carefully, meeting his gaze, knowing the time had come. 'He says he . . . wants me back.'

Jacques didn't blink, didn't move, didn't even breathe. He simply stared. Finally, knuckles whitening as he gripped the table-top, he asked very quietly, 'And what do you want, Lesley?'

The world spun on around them. Customers chattered, silverware clattered. The door banged. Tyres squealed outside in the street. But neither of them heard a thing. It was as though they existed on a different plane altogether. Lesley fancied she could hear the blood roaring in her veins, could hear the heavy thump of Jacques' heart.

Her voice, when it came, was barely a whisper, and yet she knew the words deafened him. 'I want . . . Matt.'

Jacques' jaw clenched and the colour seemed to drain from his ruddy, weathered face. She reached out to touch his hand, to offer compassion, friendship—something—*anything*. But he jerked away as if her fingers were live coals.

'Two rhubarb pies and coffee.' Kate's cheerful voice broke into the tension as she set the plates in front of them.

Lesley gave her a fleeting smile, her eyes scarcely leaving Jacques. His colour was returning already. His face was darkening, in fact. Anger, she thought. Fury. Pain.

'I'm sorry.'

Jacques didn't say anything. He picked up his fork and

leaned his elbows on the table, the fork locked in the fingers of both hands. 'I know you are.' His voice was calm, emotionless. His fingers were bending the fork in half.

'Isn't it any good, then?' a voice asked, and Lesley looked up, startled, to see Kate's worried face. 'The pie,' she added when both Lesley and Jacques looked blank.

'It's fine,' Lesley assured her. 'We're just . . . taking our time.' She gave Kate a hopeful smile which the other girl returned warily. Her gaze centred on Jacques' face, then on the fork in his hands. She gave a startled, 'Oh!' and vanished to wait on suddenly needy customers.

'I shouldn't have told you I'd marry you,' Lesley said urgently. 'It was my fault. I should never——'

'It was my fault,' Jacques said heavily. 'I should have smartened up. It's always been Colter, hasn't it, ever since you met him?'

Lesley sighed. 'Yes.'

'You think he's changed that much? You really think he'll stay around this time?'

'I don't know. But even if he leaves me, leaves our marriage, I wouldn't be good for anyone else. I couldn't be, you see.' Lesley smiled sadly. 'He's . . . spoiled me.'

Jacques grimaced.

Lesley met his gaze, saw the hurt there, would have given anything not to have been the one to cause it, wished she could ease it and yet knew she was the last person on earth who ought to try. Numbly she bowed her head and attempted to eat her pie.

Jacques made no pretence of trying to eat his. He drank his coffee, and when Lesley had done all she could to make her plate look emptier he pushed back his chair. 'I'll take you home now,' he said heavily.

He paid the bill, not even noticing when Kate smiled at him and spoke to him, and then he held the door for Lesley to go out ahead of him. They walked back to the car in silence. Jacques did not touch her again.

He didn't speak, either, until they were pulling into her driveway. Then he simply rested his hands on the bottom of the steering-wheel and said tonelessly, 'Goodbye.'

Lesley opened her mouth to say something, but had no words. 'I wish——' she began at last, but he cut her off sharply.

'Don't!'

She looked at his set jaw, his fingers clenched over the steering-wheel, and closed her mouth. He was right—there was nothing she could say. She sighed softly and, touching his shoulder for a brief instant, let herself out of the door.

He was gone before she reached the porch.

The children were in bed and Uncle Harry was chuckling his way through *Late Night with David Letterman*. But Matt was waiting for her at the bottom of the stairs, and the moment she stepped in he enfolded her in his arms. 'Are you all right?'

'You should be asking about Jacques,' Lesley said hoarsely, relishing the warm strength that wrapped her close.

Matt pressed his lips together. 'He'll survive.'

'Yes,' she agreed. 'I just feel such a rat.'

'Would it have been better to go through with marrying him?'

'No.'

'Well then . . .' he murmured against her ear. 'You did the right thing.'

'Yes,' Lesley agreed. 'But I feel like hell, just the same.'

'Come on,' he said, drawing her up the stairs with him. 'Let's go to bed.'

Matt had already showered and so he waited for her in bed, just the way he had the night before. And it felt so right to walk into the bedroom and find him there that

Lesley was stricken again by the worry about what she would do if she ever walked in and he wasn't there.

She slipped out of her robe, shut off the light and slid into bed beside him, clutching him to her almost fiercely.

He laughed softly. 'Hey, what's this?'

'I'm scared,' she admitted shakily.

He turned her in his arms. 'Scared?'

'I need you so much. I always have. I learned to get along without you once. I don't think I could do it again,' she whispered.

He stroked her hair. 'Well, relax.' He rolled her on to her back and stripped the gown over her head, then settled himself in the cradle of her thighs. 'I'm not going anywhere.'

He kissed her, moulding her body to the hard contours of his, stoking the need within her and matching it with his own. Then quite suddenly he chuckled. 'Well, that's not quite true,' he said, and she stiffened.

'Matt?'

'Shh,' he soothed her, and she could still hear the smile in his voice. 'Next weekend we all go to Newport. To see my parents.'

It wasn't the sort of news that was inclined to make Lesley relax. Matt's parents were about as far from hers as was humanly imaginable. The unstable jack-of-all-trades and the long-suffering housewife whom she had called Mom and Dad were, despite their failings, at least approachable. Career Foreign Service officer Hamilton Colter and his charity volunteer, blue-blood wife, Elizabeth, had always seemed as remote as Everest to Lesley during her life with their son.

It wasn't that they were unkind to her—far from it. They were always unfailingly polite, encouraging, and ever so expectant.

'I'm sure there must be a hospital guild you can get involved in,' Matt's mother had said to Lesley the first time they met.

'I'm in nurse's training,' Lesley reminded her.

'Yes, dear,' Elizabeth had replied absently. 'Our group redid the paediatrics wing at Newport Hospital this past year. So rewarding. You'd find it enormously fulfilling, and it will give you something to keep you busy while Matthew's away.'

Lesley had smiled and hadn't said any more to her future mother-in-law. She hadn't known then how much Matthew was going to be away. She hadn't thought that far ahead.

She spent the rest of the week thinking ahead now and fretting about what Matt's parents would say when she met them again. She'd had minimal contact with them since her separation from Matt. They hadn't sought her out, and she certainly hadn't been in touch with them. The only time she had attempted any contact with them at all came shortly after Matt was taken captive.

Then she had written them a letter from Colombia, commiserating and offering whatever support she could. She'd had back a formally printed expression of gratitude for her concern. She realised then that chances were they hadn't seen her letter at all, that it had been handled by one of Hamilton's staff or by Elizabeth's appointments secretary.

She had no real idea what they thought of her separation from Matt. She didn't know how they would feel about their getting back together. And she had absolutely no notion of how they would react to the news that they had recently been endowed with two half-grown grandchildren.

'Don't worry about it,' Matt told her.

'Did you tell them?'

'Tell them what?'

'About . . . us. About Teddy and Rita.'

'Sure.'

'What did they say?'

He shrugged. 'They said fine. They think it's a great idea. I told you, don't worry.'

But Lesley worried anyway. She was good at it, so why not? And besides, she thought as the week progressed, for all his blasé words Matt seemed to be on edge himself.

By Friday after school when they piled the children in the car, bade farewell to Uncle Harry and started south, he was clearly tense.

'Don't you want to go?' Lesley asked him.

'Of course I want to go. Why wouldn't I?' he said gruffly, knuckles white on the steering-wheel.

Lesley shrugged. 'You tell me. You just seem a bit—nervous.'

'I'm not nervous.'

'Well, I wouldn't think so,' she said easily. Matt had always had a good relationship with his parents, as far as she knew. 'It isn't as if you haven't seen them recently,' she added.

'I haven't.'

She looked at him. 'But—when you were in the hospital . . .?'

'I didn't see them.'

'You were in Washington for over a week. Your father goes down there constantly.'

'I didn't see them,' he repeated flatly. 'My father is a busy man. For all that he's retired, he doesn't spend much time at home. He's on goodness knows how many boards, commissions and such like. Half of Congress beats a path to his door.'

'Yes, but . . .' But if he said he hadn't seen them, clearly he hadn't. 'Well,' Lesley said brightly after a moment, 'no wonder you're a bit shaky. It's been a long time.'

'I'm not shaky, either!' Matt snapped with such

vehemence that she subsided into silence. Maybe shaky wasn't the word; but 'temperamental' seemed to cover it.

Lesley didn't say anything else until they were close to the Massachusetts border. Then she asked, 'Do you want me to drive?'

'No.'

'Sure?'

'I'm fine,' he snapped irritably. But before they even reached Boston he was complaining of a headache.

'Let's stop for dinner,' Lesley suggested, 'and then I'll drive.'

This time Matt didn't demur. They stopped for lobster rolls and coleslaw on the outskirts of Boston, and then, with the children well-fed, drowsy and considerably less inquisitive about these unknown grandparents, they set off again.

'Rest,' Lesley urged him, and obediently he shut his eyes. But the tenseness did not leave his face, and by the time they had reached Providence he was hunched forward in the seat, like a tortoise girding itself for attack.

Lesley found out why with five minutes of their arrival.

By Newport standards, the Colters' house was a shack, by Lesley's it was a veritable palace. The first time she had come here she'd walked around with her mouth hanging like a trap-door with the hinges sprung. She had developed a certain amount of sophistication in the intervening years, but it still had the power to intimidate her.

About as homely as the Acropolis, and about as big too, it loomed floodlit as they drove up the curving drive and pulled to a halt in front of the broad marble steps that led to the Doric-columned front porch. Not porch, Lesley corrected herself. Portico. And when the front door opened she half expected to see a Greek chorus or, at least, the Mormon Tabernacle Choir, march out to greet them. It was almost an anticlimax when only two people appeared.

Matt, who had picked up a sleepy Rita and was carrying her in his arms, stiffened as his mother descended the steps and gave him a hug and a discreet peck on the cheek.

'Matthew! It's wonderful to see you.'

He smiled and brushed her cheek with his lips. 'You too, Mom.'

'I'm so sorry I couldn't make it down to Washington to see you while you were in the hospital. It was in May, you know. We always do the homeless benefit in May.'

'I know . . .' he began, but she went right on.

'You look marvellously fit, in any case. You must be dying to go back.'

Matt didn't confirm or deny that. He just smiled vaguely and accepted his father's hearty handshake.

'Good to see you, son.'

Hamilton Colter was an older, steelier version of his son. He had the same stubborn jaw, the same penetrating stare, and he fixed it on his son now, assessing him and finally making a judgement. 'Your mother's right, you are looking good. I knew you would. Colters weather anything. Knew you'd be up and at 'em in no time. That's my boy!'

Matt didn't say anything, and finally Lesley had to.

'Speaking of boys,' she said, reaching Matt's side with Teddy in tow, 'we'd like you to meet our son. And our daughter,' she added as Matt deposited Rita on the steps and kept his hands protectively on her shoulders. 'This is Teddy, and this is Rita.'

'Charming,' said Elizabeth, tipping Rita's chin up and smiling down at her. 'What a pretty girl you are!' She turned her gaze on Teddy. 'And what a handsome boy! I'm sure you'll be a credit to your parents.'

'Yes'm,' Teddy said. Rita simply stared.

'Come in, come in.' Elizabeth herded them up the steps and into the echoing foyer with its marble floors and wainscoting and its crystal chandelier. 'Make yourselves at home.'

Teddy rolled his eyes and Lesley put her hand over her mouth to hide a smile.

'Nice lad,' Mr Colter said to Lesley as Teddy stared around. 'Stands straight, he does. I like that. Shows he's got confidence. He'll do well.'

'Yes,' Lesley agreed, though not certain the posture had anything to do with it. 'I think he will.'

'Like Matt,' his father went on. 'And me, and my father before me.' He hurried on to catch up with his son, and Lesley heard him say, 'I see they caught those bastards who grabbed you. A couple of them, anyway.'

Matt nodded.

'Thank heaven! Think of the articles you can get out of that. When are you leaving?'

'Oh, don't let's talk about that now, Hamilton,' Mrs Colter chided him, shooing them all into a sitting-room at the back of the house. 'Matthew's only just got here. Come along, Lesley. Carrie will show you where I've put the children. Perhaps you'll want to see them off to bed. Then you and Matt can come back down and have a nice chat with us.' As she spoke, she nodded at the older woman who had appeared as if by magic to smile at them. Lesley remembered her as the woman who'd been their live-in help when Matt had brought her here the first time.

'That would be fine.' But, before she could follow the older woman up the stairs, Matt hauled Rita back up into his arms and said, 'I'll take 'em. I think I might hit the sack too—I'm tired. See you in the morning.'

Elizabeth Colter looked a bit astonished at Matt's annoucement, and Hamilton said, 'I thought we'd have a brandy and talk, Matt.'

But Matt shook his head. 'Tomorrow. OK, Dad? I'm beat.'

Hamilton looked at him narrowly, and seemed about to protest when Elizabeth cut in, 'Whatever you want, dear.'

'Fair enough,' said Hamilton, clapping Matt on the shoulder. 'See you bright and early. We've got a lot of catching up to do.'

Matt nodded. 'You coming, Les?'

Did he have to ask?

For nothing on earth did Lesley want to remain downstairs with both Matthew's formidable parents looking expectantly at her. If he didn't think it the height of rudeness to arrive and go promptly off to bed, who was to disagree? 'Yes, I am.'

She gave Elizabeth and Hamilton what she hoped was a bright, competent smile, since her experience was that Matt's parents appreciated shining competence above all else, and said, 'I do hope you'll excuse us.'

'Yes, dear, go ahead,' Elizabeth replied. 'You and I will have plenty of time for a chat in the morning. I'm sure Hamilton will have Matthew tied up for hours and hours.'

Hamilton did.

It was cloudy and late when Lesley awoke. Matt was no longer in bed beside her. She rolled over in the big bed and felt suddenly bereft at the absence of the hard warmth of his body next to hers. He had scarcely spoken a word after they had got the children down to bed in rooms directly across the hall from their own. But when she had put the light out and slid into bed beside him, expecting to be cuddled in his arms while he went promptly off to sleep, she found she was mistaken.

In less time than it had taken her to put her nightgown on, Matt had it off again.

'Matthew,' she had protested. 'Your parents!'

He had raised his head and looked around the darkened room. 'Where?'

'Not here, idiot,' Lesley had laughed. 'But they might hear.'

'They won't. Their bedroom is on the other side of the earth.' Which, Lesley realised, wasn't stretching things much.

'But——'

'Shhh,' he had muttered, silencing her with persuasive lips. 'Love me. Now.'

And moments later, when he had joined himself to her, he'd lifted his lips from hers long enough to whisper, 'Oh, Les, I need you!' and showed her with a desperation that surprised her just how much.

He awakened her again that night and loved her just as passionately. His need had been intense, his joining urgent, and afterwards, when he'd slept, he'd still clung to her as if she were a buoy in a stormswept sea.

When she awoke in the morning, however, she drifted alone. Yawning and stretching, still wondering at the fervour of Matt's lovemaking, she rose and pulled back the curtains to look out over broad lawns and neatly sculptured gardens.

A far cry from the jumbled garden and patchy lawn of Uncle Harry's house, the Colters' grounds were all very neat, predictable and controlled. But beyond them, shrouded now in morning mist, Lesley could just make out the sea. At least that was the same. Even Newport's wealth and power couldn't control it. She smiled and went to get dressed.

She hoped to find Matt and take a walk with him. While quite a lot of Newport—its fancy mansions and its yachts—daunted her, she loved the Cliff Walk. It wound along the coast with the great mansion summerhouses on one side and the rolling sea on the other. Whenever she and Matt had come here, that was always where they went.

She peeped into the children's rooms on the way to look

for him, and they, too, had apparently gone downstairs. It wasn't hard to find them, though. From the hallway she could make out Rita's shrill, childish tones in the kitchen as she regaled Florrie, the cook, with accounts of life in second grade. And when she got there she could see Teddy outside with his grandmother, being given a guided tour around the grounds.

'Good morning, Mrs Lesley.' Florrie motioned her into a chair and poured her a cup of coffee. 'I hope you slept well.'

'Very, thank you,' Lesley replied, sitting down and pulling Rita into her lap for a quick hug. 'And now I'm looking forward to going for a walk. I wonder if you've seen Matt?'

'He's in the study with Mr Colter,' Florrie told her. 'Been in there since early. You want eggs and ham or cereal, Mrs Lesley?'

Ultimately it didn't matter what Lesley wanted, she got everything Florrie had going.

'You need fattening up,' Florrie decreed, piling the food on Lesley's plate. She was still standing over the younger woman, watching her eat, when Elizabeth and Teddy came back inside.

'Have you been out there, Mama?' Teddy's dark eyes shone. 'It's about the biggest garden I've ever seen!'

Lesley smiled. 'Yes, I have. It's lovely. I was just going to go for a walk. I thought I'd get Matt to come with me.'

Elizabeth shook her head. 'Oh, why don't you just take the children, my dear?' she suggested. 'I'm sure he and his father are still talking.'

'I could wait,' said Lesley.

'Do we have to?' Teddy asked. 'Let's just go. Please!'

Lesley was torn. She wanted to wait for Matt, but she didn't want to sit there and make small talk with her mother-in-law for an indeterminate time either. At last she shrugged apologetically. 'If you don't mind,' she said to

Elizabeth, 'I'll just take them a short way.'

'I don't mind at all. I think it's wonderful what you're doing,' the older woman said, giving Rita a pat on the head and Lesley a beneficent smile that the younger woman found frankly puzzling. 'Besides, I'm sure Matt will want to fill his father in. They have a great deal to discuss.'

Lesley wondered how much Matt would tell his father. He had told her next to nothing about his captivity. All her subtle and not-so-subtle attempts to find out what had gone on then had been soundly rebuffed.

Generally he could sleep now because she slept with him. And if occasionally he awoke, crying out, her arms around him always soothed him so that he could sleep again.

Of what he dreamt, of what he thought or felt or remembered, he said no word to her.

But he had always idolised his father. Ever since she'd met Matt she had heard how fine a man Hamilton Colter was, how talented a diplomat, how outstanding a public servant, how hard Matt worked to live up to him. Maybe, she thought enviously, Matt would find in his father the confidant he had never found in her.

Lesley took the children on a far longer walk than she had intended. As long as Matt was with his father, she had nothing to go back for. And there was always one more mansion to see, one more bend to round, one more indescribable view to appreciate and, for Teddy at least, one more rocky precipice to scramble around on.

But finally Rita tired and Lesley said, 'Come on, now, it's time to go back. Lunch is always served at twelve-thirty, and if we hurry we might make it.'

They hurried, the children suddenly ravenous, and Lesley hoping to find Matt at the table. But there was only her mother-in-law waiting when they got back.

Elizabeth shrugged. 'They're still at it,' she explained, with a nod towards the closed study door. Lesley's eyebrows went up, then down. Obviously Matt had told all. She felt a fleeting jealousy, then banished it and sent the children off to wash their hands. She hoped they would behave as well during lunch as they had in their new grandmother's presence that morning and the night before.

Happily, they did. And after the meal they bounced off to play ball on the long, sloping lawn that looked out over the cliffs, leaving Lesley alone with her mother-in-law.

Florrie cleared away the dishes and brought out a fresh pot of tea. Elizabeth smiled and urged Lesley to move to the sofa so that it overlooked the lawn where the children played, and then offered her a cup of tea.

Lesley cast about for some suitable small talk. Something—anything—that she and her mother-in-law might have in common. There wasn't much, besides Matt.

But before she could come up with anything Elizabeth said bluntly, 'I'm quite relieved that you and Matthew have patched up your difficulties.'

Lesley blinked. She had always suspected that Elizabeth could cut right to the heart of any matter she wished, but it was still a surprise when it happened.

'I must say,' Elizabeth went on, 'I wasn't really surprised when I heard you'd separated. I told Hamilton when you two married, "That girl doesn't know what she's getting into." I was sure you didn't know what kind of man Matthew was, wouldn't understand him.' Elizabeth stirred her tea, then reached out and patted her daughter-in-law's knee. 'But I see now that you do.'

Lesley raised her eyebrows slightly, wondering how her mother-in-law had deduced this.

'You must, of course,' Elizabeth said firmly. 'I knew it the moment Matthew told me about the children.'

Lesley's brows rose even higher.

Her mother-in-law sipped her tea and smiled her approval. 'It was such a generous thing to do, taking on a project like that.'

Lesley swallowed her astonishment. 'I didn't do it to be generous,' she blurted.

Elizabeth looked at her quizzically. 'Oh, but my dear——'

'I could never have done anything else.'

Elizabeth's cup rattled in her saucer. 'But surely——'

Lesley leaned forward earnestly. 'Teddy and Rita were my friends,' she tried to explain. 'I knew their mother, their grandmother. After the earthquake, they were alone. We were all alone,' she added softly, staring out across the lawn, unseeing, remembering how she had needed them just as desperately as they had needed her.

Elizabeth just looked at her, as if Lesley were speaking a foreign tongue. Then at last she set her cup down in its Limoges saucer and murmured, 'Oh, my dear!' as if Lesley had just confessed to some terrible weakness.

Then she looked out of the window to where the children were scampering away behind the trees, made a tsking sound and shook her head.

Lesley, dumbfounded, couldn't say a word.

Happily she didn't have to, for Elizabeth was never one to linger on a delicate topic. She was too well-bred for that. Instead she launched directly into a long monologue about the charity ball she was helping to arrange for the benefit of a region-wide crippled children's organisation.

Lesley was required to do no more than nod and make affirmative noises whenever Elizabeth showed signs of winding down. Periodically she cast longing glances at the closed door to Hamilton's study, wondering just what Matt was saying or hearing in there, wishing she could simply walk in and say, 'Get me out of this place.' But she couldn't, of course.

The conversation didn't get back to a personal level for almost an hour. And then Elizabeth said, 'When is Matthew leaving again?'

'Leaving?'

'Going back to work.'

'Oh.' Lesley stirred her tea, which was by this time stone-cold in her cup. 'I . . . don't think he's go . . . I mean, he's working now.'

'Now?' Elizabeth regarded her sharply.

'He's doing some writing on his own. And he's working with my uncle Harry—you remember him. When he retired, he took over the newspaper in Day's Harbor.'

Elizabeth looked at her incredulously. 'Matthew is working for him?'

'Not *for* him precisely. *With* him. Doing articles, proof-reading, editing. Even some printing.'

Elizabeth gave a little laugh. 'Oh, yes. But surely that's just while he's recuperating.'

Lesley gave an awkward little shrug. 'He . . . says not.'

Elizabeth sat up straight. 'Nonsense! He has obligations, commitments—responsibilities.' She gave Lesley a hard look, as if expecting her to add to the litany.

Lesley, worried, didn't say a word.

Elizabeth put her saucer down on the table and stood up. She prowled restlessly about the room, glanced distractedly at the closed door to the study, then at Lesley. Finally she came to an abrupt stop in front of Lesley. 'He can't be serious!' she exclaimed.

'I don't know,' Lesley allowed, because it was only the truth.

Her mother-in-law gave a little disbelieving shake of her head, then, such treason apparently incomprehensible, she said, 'I'm sure he was only saying that, my dear. Matthew knows his real responsibilities, his real focus in life. He wouldn't waste everything mouldering away up there in a dank little lobster town in Maine, now would he?'

And Lesley wondered just what she was expected to answer to that.

CHAPTER NINE

WHAT his parents thought was as clear as the plate-glass expanse of windows that extended across the back of the house. If Elizabeth could be considered even remotely circumspect about her opinion, Hamilton definitely could not.

He had his arm slung around Matt's shoulders when they finally emerged from the study late that afternoon, and he was saying cheerfully, 'I can see it now. Best damn series of articles you could hope for. Eyewitness inside and out. You'll get a Pulitzer out of it at least, or I'll eat my hat.'

'I don't know, Dad,' said Matt, easing out from beneath his father's arm. 'There's more to a Pulitzer than being an eyewitness.'

'Of course there is, boy. I know that,' Hamilton said bluffly. 'But you've got that too—style, intensity, power. You've proved that. Hasn't he, Lesley?' Like an eagle he zoomed in on Lesley, who was sitting on the sofa trying to read a book while her mother-in-law made countless phone calls encouraging people to drop in and say hello to Matt tonight.

'He's . . . very talented,' said Lesley, trapped once again into not being able to say what she felt. She looked closely at Matt, hoping to discern what he felt. But he seemed closed off, shuttered. As remote as he had looked when she'd seen him interviewed or when he'd first come home.

'Of course he is,' Elizabeth chipped in. 'He's our son.'

Matt was heading for the door and she scurried after him. 'Don't run off now,' she chastised him. 'We've been planning a little party to celebrate your return. Just a few of our close friends. And there'll be a few friends stopping by for brunch tomorrow.'

'Ma——'

'I know you're not fond of parties, Matthew. But you have to give people a chance to give you a hero's welcome home.'

'I'm not a damn hero!'

Elizabeth took a step backwards at his vehemence. But then she drew herself up with the regal sternness Lesley always expected of her and said firmly, 'False modesty doesn't become you, Matthew. These people are our closest friends. They will expect you to be there tonight. Your father and I will expect you to be there.'

Their gazes battled for interminable seconds. Then Matt shoved his hands into his pockets and nodded. Without a word, without a sign to Lesley, he turned then and stalked out of the room.

Lesley stared after him, a hollow feeling growing where her stomach used to be.

Hamilton waited until the front door slammed, then shook his head. 'He's damned touchy. Sometimes I wonder if I know him any more.'

'Nonsense,' Elizabeth said briskly, picking up the phone again. 'Matthew's always been prickly, but he's still our son. He'll do what's expected of him. He always does.'

The notion made Lesley ill.

She wished Matt were around to counter it, to tell her that his mother was wrong. But he wasn't.

He had taken off without so much as a backward glance, without a flicker of remembrance of her or the children.

It shouldn't have surprised her. If nothing else, this weekend had certainly taught her why Matt was the way he was.

He was, pure and simple, his parents' son.

He didn't think about individuals any more than they

did.

To see Teddy and Rita as a 'project', to think of the homeless as an 'issue', to consider child abuse merely an abstract 'problem' was as foreign to Lesley as her narrower, more specific way of life was to Hamilton and Elizabeth Colter.

They cared—of course they did. Lesley would never have denied that.

But Hamilton and Elizabeth Colter cared on a grand scale, a scale that endowed whole wings of hospitals or raised thousands of dollars for causes. The particular people afflicted were not personally important to them. As individuals they were only indicative of the larger problem, not an end in themselves.

And, for all her fond dreams, could she really expect him to change? How could she honestly expect him to remain there? Wasn't she deluding herself?

As Elizabeth pointed out, there wasn't much of the world in sight from Day's Harbor.

It was all too clear how Matt's parents felt. Would Hamilton change? Would Elizabeth? Of course not. They saw no reason to.

And, most likely, after an afternoon with his father, neither would Matt. He had already forgotten her existence.

Lesley's eyes blurred as she looked out towards the horizon. It was going to be harder to let go than she had ever imagined. Starting to love him again was going to prove every bit as painful as she had feared.

Hamilton and Elizabeth Colter turned out to have somewhere between a hundred and a hundred and twenty 'close friends'. After a while, Lesley lost count. It didn't matter anyway, because she couldn't keep any of them straight, and they were only marginally interested in meeting her.

The children were a novelty. She was praised roundly for her compassion and her charity for having adopted them. She managed this time to contain her impulse to correct them. She simply smiled and nodded and privately counted the hours until she could make a graceful escape.

Matt hadn't even made a graceful entrance yet.

They ate an early cold supper without him. Hamilton harumphed at his son's absence, and Elizabeth pursed her lips in displeasure. Teddy and Rita wanted to know where he was and why he hadn't taken them with him. And Lesley maintained an almost complete silence because she didn't know the answers, and because she had worries and questions enough of her own.

She was glad she had thought to put in a party dress for Rita and a clean pair of khaki trousers and a sports shirt for Teddy, as well as a dressy pale blue scoop-neck sheath for herself. They at least didn't look too out of place as the main rooms of the Colter mansion gradually filled with elegantly dressed women and men in evening clothes.

They felt out of place, though. Because Matt wasn't with them.

'Where's your hero husband?' one tall, imposing woman in a glittering rose-coloured dress asked Lesley after they had been introduced.

'I expect he'll be along shortly,' Lesley replied, crossing her fingers, privately furious with him. This was his scene, after all. *She* didn't belong here. And Teddy and Rita certainly didn't.

As adaptable as Teddy and Rita had become, they were still eager to go upstairs to watch television instead of being the centre of attraction. But, though Lesley was ready to let them go, Hamilton wasn't through with them yet.

Perhaps it was because Matt was still absent, or perhaps it was because he wanted to make the point to her and the children that he had obviously made to Matt earlier in the day, but he left his cronies by the bar long enough to corral Lesley and the children just before she was going to send them upstairs, and proceeded to focus all his urbane civility and charm on them. In short order, Lesley could see why he'd been such a success as a diplomat.

'These people are all delighted to meet you, you know,' he said to the children. 'They think you're pretty special. They think your father's pretty special too. He is. He's a hero,' he told Teddy grandly, looping an arm over the boy's thin shoulders. 'Not many men could survive what he has.'

'I know,' Teddy agreed with pride.

'But even before his escape, he gave something important to the world. For years people all over the English-speaking world have benefited from his insights into world situations,' Hamilton went on. 'Do you realise that?'

Teddy nodded. 'His writing, you mean?'

'Exactly. He's won two Pulitzers, you know.'

'What's a Pul-it-zer? asked Rita.

'A prize,' her grandfather told her. 'A very important national prize.'

Rita's eyes got big and round. 'Like for a spelling-bee? My friend Patsy won our class spelling-bee this year.'

Hamilton smiled. 'Good for Patsy. Yes, it's like a spelling-bee, but even more important.'

Rita looked suitably awed. 'Gosh!'

'Exactly.' Hamilton hunkered down so that he was on Rita's level. 'When a person can spell like your friend Patsy, she ought to, right?'

Both children nodded.

'It's a talent, a gift. You understand?'

'Uh-huh.'

'And it isn't right to be selfish with one's own gifts, is it?'

Both of them shook their heads.

'And it isn't right to be selfish with another's either, is it?'

This time they both looked confused until their grandfather elaborated. 'I mean,' Hamilton said, 'that your father has obligations, responsibilities to the world beyond your family. He has an important job—a gift—an ability to write, and he ought to go back to it as soon as possible, don't you agree?'

They both nodded again.

'And you, my dear,' he said, rising to his full height again and rounding on Lesley as she stood staring out of the window, marvelling at his skill. 'Surely you can't mean to limit him?'

'Me?' Lesley turned and stared.

'Why else would he be writing on Harry's toy paper?' Hamilton scoffed. 'You surely don't imagine that will satisfy him for long?'

Lesley took a deep breath, but before she could say a word, Hamilton went on, 'Think about what's best for him, what's best for the world, my dear.' His powerful arm gave her shoulders a quick squeeze. 'I'm sure his experience has confused him, unsettled him. But together we must make him see sense. I can count on you, can't I?'

Fortunately, before Lesley had to give an answer, Elizabeth appeared at Hamilton's side and spirited him away. 'Ambassador Stenner just came in, darling,' she said. 'I know you'll want to speak with him. You will excuse us, won't you, Lesley?' she said over her shoulder. 'Why don't you be a dear and see if you can find Matt?'

This last was spoken with rather more desperation than Lesley suspected her mother-in-law usually displayed. But his absence, at first overlooked, was now becoming more of a topic of conversation. His wife was here. His children was here. Where was the hero of the hour?

Lesley knew no more than anyone else. But she was glad of the suggestion that she search. It gave her a chance to escape the unrelenting scrutiny of the United States' power and élite who were the Colters' friends.

She herded the children upstairs, oversaw their night-time ablutions, then settled them in the TV room with strict instructions to behave, be quiet, and be in bed by ten o'clock. Then she went in search of Matt.

His father had already found him in the breakfast-room, still attired in the casual cords and polo shirt he had worn earlier in the day. 'Where the hell have you been?' he demanded.

'Out.'

'Obviously. Well, now you're back, and we have a houseful of people waiting to talk to you. At least Lesley and the children know what's expected of them as Colters. They were here.'

Matt's eyes met hers across the room. He looked wary, hunted almost. Lesley looked back at him the same way. Where had he been? More importantly, why hadn't he taken her with him? The rapport they had been building seemed to have vanished into thin air.

'Good for them,' said Matt, his voice tinged with bitterness. He threw his shoulders back and raked his fingers through his hair. 'I'll get cleaned up and be right back down.'

He brushed past Lesley without a word, and disappeared up the back stairs.

The rest of the evening got steadily worse. Matt was back in less than twenty minutes, looking polished and presentable in a dark suit, sparkling white shirt and subdued tie. He looked as if he fitted right in too. He shook hands, made small talk, deflected personal comments and adulation, and generally made his parents proud.

He made Lesley miserable.

She was losing him—she was sure of it. And why not?

She had been a fool to think that he would be satisfied to live out his life in her narrow little corner of the world. And it was no wonder he had grown increasingly remote as the day wore on.

He was probably trying to figure out how to break the news to her.

He wouldn't want to be cruel. He wouldn't want to be abrupt. After all, in all probability he must have honestly thought he would stay with her. She doubted that his deception had been intentional. If it was a deception at all, she suspected he'd been as deceived as she'd been.

And now?

Now he would have to let her down gently. The very thought made her throat tighten, made her eyes ache and sting, made her the worst possible company for a hundred well-wishers whose only thought was to encourage Matt on the road back to what he did best.

Finally she couldn't take it any longer and excused herself, pleading a headache. Lord knew, it wasn't a lie. Her head was pounding fiercely as she escaped up the stairs to bed.

She pretended to sleep when Matt came in two hours later. She felt him slip into the bed next to her and longed to have him take her in his arms, yet at the same time she feared it. Loving him when she was losing him might be the end of her.

She couldn't risk it.

And apparently Matt couldn't either, for he made no move to touch her. He was still lying beside her, rigidly awake, when she drifted into an uneasy sleep.

A none-too-gentle shaking woke her. 'Come on,' Matt was saying. 'I know you're tired, but we're leaving.'

Lesley opened one eye, squinting at him, surprised to find him leaning over her, fully dressed, when the clock behind him only said six-thirty and he hadn't come to bed until almost two. 'Wha——' she began.

'We're leaving.'

'But I thought your mother said something about a brunch.'

'We're not staying for brunch.' He was tossing clothes in the suitcase as he spoke. 'Come on. Get the kids up, will you?'

Lesley sat up, watching him warily, noting a contained violence in his movements, wondering at it. Maybe he wasn't going to let her down gently at all. Maybe he was fed up with her. Maybe he was going to drive them back to Day's Harbor and dump them as fast as he could.

'What's going on, Matthew?' she asked quietly.

'I want to leave. Now.' He didn't stop packing. He didn't even turn around. If anything, he moved faster than ever, picking up her blue sheath and flinging it on top of his crumpled white shirt, then slamming the lid of the case down on both.

It wasn't time for discussion, Lesley could see that.

She swung her legs out of bed and got up. 'Let me get a quick shower,' she said dully, 'and then I'll get the kids ready to go.'

She didn't have to. Matt saw to it while she was bathing.

'How come we're leaving, Mama?' Rita wanted to know when Lesley came into her room to braid her hair.

'Dad—er—Matt wants to.' They would have to go back to thinking of him as Matt. It would be easier on them. It would have been easier on them, she thought bitterly, if he had never come back to them at all.

'I like it here,' Rita said thoughtfully. 'But I don't think Daddy does.'

Lesley didn't know what Matt thought. That was the whole problem. 'Don't worry about it,' she counselled her daughter. 'Hold still now or your hair will pull.'

Matt had loaded the car and was leaning against the bonnet, waiting impatiently when she and Rita came down.

'Ready?' he asked tersely.

'I need to say goodbye to your parents.'

'I wrote them a note.'

Lesley stared at him. 'You didn't talk to them?'

'They aren't up.'

'Well, surely we should wait then and——'

'No.'

'But——'

'You can write them a note too, when we get home,' Matt said. 'Thank them for their hospitality and all that.' Once more she heard a hard edge to his voice that made her look at him narrowly.

He met her gaze almost defiantly, and she sighed, unwilling to question him now in front of the children.

'Very well,' she said. 'Let's go.' And she urged the children into the back seat before she climbed into the front beside Matt.

'Will we be coming back soon?' Rita asked him as he put the car in gear and started down the driveway.

Lesley looked at him out of the corner of her eye. His jaw tightened and she wished Rita hadn't asked that. How would he tell her that he would be walking out of their lives very shortly to resume his old one, and that chances were these particular grandchildren would never see these particular grandparents again?

'I don't know when we'll be back,' Matt said in answer to Rita's question. 'I suspect that will be up to them.'

'I hope it's soon,' said Teddy. 'I'd like to explore some more of those beaches. I only got to the first one.'

'Don't hold your breath,' Lesley heard Matt say quietly, and she shut her eyes against the pain of it.'

The long drive home was an endurance test. Neither she nor Matt spoke more than fifty words the whole way. He seemed tense and preoccupied, more so even than he had been on the way down. And Lesley was far from feeling jolly herself.

There must have been the sale of the century going at L. L. Bean, Lesley decided, because the Sunday traffic headed north was outrageous. They got caught in a terrific snarl on Route 95 just west of Boston that effectively slowed them down for over an hour and made the children more restless than ever. Matt snapped at them, then demanded that Lesley do something. But Lesley couldn't. She knew the task of the creative mother was to do something to distract them, yet she was wholly unable to make herself do it. She was too out of sorts herself, too preoccupied, too overwrought at the notion that in hours or, at best, days Matt would be dumping them and going back to his old life.

They ate a late lunch in Portsmouth, and whether it was the food or the fact that then they crossed the Maine state line, Lesley couldn't have said, but Matt suddenly seemed in a better mood.

He joked with Teddy and teased Rita gently about some bit of silliness that didn't even make Lesley crack a smile. She was glad someone was happy. Maybe, she thought sourly, that meant Matt had finally figured out how he was going to break the news to her and, that settled, he felt comfortable enough to enjoy his last few days with the children.

She didn't enjoy anything, and Matt commented on it more than once.

'I should have thought you'd be glad to get home,' he said to her as they drove through Portland which was, as far as Lesley was concerned, the beginning of the last lap to Day's Harbor.

'Why?' she asked testily.

He shrugged. 'I just didn't think my folks' crowd were your type.'

'I'm not good enough, you mean?'

He gave her a sharp look. 'Hey, I'm not saying that. I just meant it wasn't your usual sort of haunt.'

'No,' Lesley said irritably, 'it certainly isn't a clone of Day's Harbor.'

He slowed the car. 'What's the matter?'

'Nothing.' She stared resolutely out of the window.

'Les.' His voice was low, demanding.

'Not now,' she snapped. 'Not here.' Her gaze swung momentarily towards the children in the back seat.

Matt looked at her, baffled. Then he shrugged and turned on the radio for the rest of the drive home.

Harry was delighted to see them. 'Have a good time?' he asked Lesley.

She shrugged. 'Not bad.'

'How about you?' He turned to Matt.

Matt was equally non-committal, but the children were effusive, telling Harry all about their grandparents, the house, the garden, the Cliff Walk, and the Saturday night party.

'Sounds like somebody enjoyed it at least,' he commented, studying Matt and Lesley sagely. 'Thought you'd be back late.'

'Nope.' Matt dropped the suitcases inside the back door. 'I've got work to do here. I wanted to get busy on it. Think I'll walk down to the newspaper office now, in fact.'

The words were barely out of his mouth before he'd turned and headed back down the steps. Aching inside, Lesley watched him go.

She didn't really have a chance to talk to him until they had gone upstairs to go to bed. He hadn't come back from the office until suppertime, and afterwards he had played cards with the children and had chatted with Harry. She had avoided him, unable to pretend that everything was all right while she waited for the axe to drop.

But there was no way to avoid him once he shut the

bedroom door. And there was no way to avoid the pain that she knew would follow whatever words he spoke in an effort to make her feel better.

It would be best if he just got it over with. Said it right out. She would rather face a clean, sharp decision to leave, followed by his leaving at once, than have him tiptoe around her feelings while their new relationship bled slowly to death.

Accordingly she shut the door and leaned against it, her arms folded across her chest as if they might somehow protect her from the blow.

'So, say it,' she said.

Matt paused, his shirt half over his head, and peered at her over the top of the collar. 'Say what?'

'Don't pretend, Matt. I'm not blind.'

A crease appeared between his brows. He jerked the shirt over his head and tossed it on the bed. 'What are you talking about?'

Lesley clenched her fists. Damn him! 'I know you're going!'

He blinked. 'Going?'

'Oh, hell!' she exploded. 'Why don't you just get it over with? Tell me you've changed your mind—I can take it. Just stop playing games with me!'

He looked at her warily, then crossed the room, his bare feet soundless on the carpet. He took her by the arms and looked down into her eyes. 'Let me get this straight. You think I'm leaving you?'

'Of course I think you're leaving me,' she said shrilly. 'Oh, not just me—Maine, the kids. All this!' She tried to make a sweeping motion with her arm, but he held her fast, his fingers gripping her tightly. 'How could you not? It's your job. It's what your parents expect. It's what everyone expects. It's what Matthew Colter has been groomed since birth to do!'

A corner of his mouth lifted slightly. 'And that's why you've been bitchy all day? Because you thought I was going?'

Lesley glared at him. 'Because you are going,' she corrected him stonily.

He shook his head. 'I'm not, you know,' he said almost casually.

It was her turn to blink, then to suspect her hearing was failing. 'Huh?'

'You're wrong. And you're stuck with me. There is no place on earth I'd rather be, Lesley Colter, and no place on earth I intend to be, but right here in Maine with you.'

CHAPTER TEN

'I DON'T understand,' Lesley said numbly. 'Your father——'

'My father wants me to fly out to Batar tonight. Hell, he wanted me to fly out three weeks ago, the second I got out of the hospital. It's what he would do. It's what he expects me to do.' Matt paused and looked at her squarely. 'But I'm not going to do it.'

Lesley felt as if her mind was reeling, as if her heart had taken a roller-coaster ride. 'You're . . . I mean, you told him that?'

Matt sighed and shook his head. 'Not exactly. I considered it. I thought I would. In the end, I didn't.'

'But——'

'That's why we left when we did.'

All of a sudden she began to laugh. Over and over his words echoed in her head, 'There's no place on earth I intend to be, but right here with you.' And she laughed. Smiled. Giggled. Went giddy with relief. She felt as if she had climbed Everest without oxygen and couldn't find even one lungful of rarified air. And she loved every minute of it.

'You mean it, don't you?' she said when she could speak at last.

'Of course I mean it,' Matt said gruffly. He was undressing her frantically, and she began to do the same to him. Fingers fumbled, zippers rasped, buttons slid free. Shirts and jeans tangled in a heap on the floor. It became almost a race, their desperate need to reaffirm their belonging to each other driving them.

The well of Lesley's despair filled now with joy, and she

came to him, laughing and sobbing. And Matt matched her desperation, seeking and, she hoped, finding in their sharing the affirmation of her love for him.

Finally, spent, Matt rolled her on top of him and linked his arms possessively across her back. 'You were really worried?' he asked softly between gentle nibbles on her chin and lower lip.

'Yes,' Lesley admitted, still able to conjure up the dreadful emptiness she had felt as the notion that he would be leaving her soon had been borne in upon her.

'I must have really done a number on you,' he said sadly.

'I'm sorry,' Lesley whispered.

He shook his head. 'I'm the one who's sorry. I think maybe we ought to get away just for the weekend, so I can work on proving myself to you. What do you think about that?'

Lesley drew her tongue slowly across her top lip, thinking. Remembering. There had been other weekends. She remembered them well. They had never got through one of them without Matt being called away. The very thought could send her into a panic.

But maybe he was right. If they went, and if they managed to get through it, maybe then she would be able to trust him completely. Maybe then she wouldn't panic at the slightest hint that every promise he made was nothing more than hot air.

'All right,' she agreed.

'This weekend?'

'Yes—wait! No, I can't. I have to go to Boston.'

'So I'll go too.'

'But——'

'Why not?' He smiled up at her. 'I'd want to go anyway, and this way we'll only be imposing on Harry's generosity once.'

'I'll have to go to some workshops. I have to give a talk.'

He shrugged. 'No problem. I can find plenty to do. What do you say?'

She said, 'I'd like that.'

Boston was Boston—historical, hard-driving, hectic, and Lesley had never loved it more.

It wasn't the city, of course, though that too was as enchanting as always. It was having Matt by her side.

They drove down early on Friday morning with Harry's blessing. 'Stay as long as you want,' he had said magnanimously as he and the children waved them off. 'You two have got a powerful lot of catchin' up t'do.'

It wouldn't be all 'catching up', of course. Lesley's conference would demand a good chunk of her time. But there would be time for the two of them too. Matt had promised her that. And when she'd daringly suggested that he might like to drop in at the *Worldview* offices in Boston, he had declined at once.

'No way.'

Lesley didn't question him further. She turned her attention to other things, like how much fun it was to walk arm in arm down Newbury Street with him, pausing along the way to window-shop and, later in the afternoon, to have tea at the Ritz.

'I can't believe I'm doing this,' she mumbled through a mouthful of buttered muffin, her eyes darting about, taking in the entire setting, memorising every detail for later mulling.

Matt grinned at her. 'We could have stayed here. I didn't realise you'd get quite so turned on.'

Lesley laughed. 'It isn't the Ritz that's turning me on,' she assured him, and made his grin widen further. 'Besides, I need to be where the conference is when it starts tonight.'

'We can do it another time, then,' he promised.

And her faith in him had grown to the extent that she

didn't automatically feel a twinge of doubt at his words. She smiled and thought, yes, I'd like that, another time.

Before they went to the conference reception that evening, they ate dinner at a trendy seafood restaurant in the lower level of another one of Boston's finest hotels. Lesley had a *calamari* salad which Matt said looked like a combination of Teddy's toy wall walkers and lettuce. He, in an uncharacteristically cautious move, ordered broiled swordfish and a baked potato. Lesley chided him about his lack of adventurousness, and he just grinned.

'I'm saving myself for the things that matter,' he promised her.

That night in bed he showed her what he meant.

Afterwards she lay in his arms, listening to the muted murmur of street traffic over the steady hum of the air-conditioning, and marvelled that she was here—that he was here.

'Have you talked to your father?' She placed a hand on his chest, then nestled more deeply into the crook of his shoulder. She hadn't asked Matt about his parents since the day they had got home. He had thrown himself into work at Harry's newspaper office all week, and when he was around in the evenings there always seemed to be other people around and other things to say. She got the feeling he wanted it that way, at least for the moment. So she didn't press. But now they were alone, and they had, as Harry had said, some 'catching up' to do. In the secure warmth of each other's arms, she thought they could start on it.

'Yeah.' Matt's arm tightened around her and his other hand came up to hold hers.

Outside, fire engines and police cars wailed, coming nearer, then passed and faded slowly away. Inside, Lesley turned Matt's hand over in hers and traced the outline of his fingers with one of her own. 'You told him?'

'I told him.'

'He's upset.'

'You could say that.' Matt grimaced slightly. 'Chewed the hell out of me. Yakked on and on about my "responsibilities". My "commitments". I told him I had responsibilities and commitments here! You, the kids, Harry!'

'I don't suppose you convinced him.'

Matt gave a half-laugh and shook his head. 'Hardly. It isn't his style.'

'No, I could see that when we were there. He thinks about the big picture. The epic with the cast of thousands, not the two part play. It's not wrong, really.'

'It can be,' Matt argued. 'It can be a cop-out. It can be an excuse for not caring, while it blinds you to what's really important. Only he calls it heroism.' The laugh came again, bitter this time.

Remembering how sensitive he was about the label, Lesley kept silent. There were still things she didn't know about this man, secrets unshared, depths unplumbed. But her trust in him and her understanding of him were growing daily. He was not the man who had walked away from her two and a half years ago. He was not the man who hadn't wanted even to talk to her when she came after him.

Lesley lifted her head and kissed him on the mouth, then snuggled down once more in his embrace and slept, convinced at last that their future together was secure.

She got up at seven to shower and do her hair before she went to the opening session of the conference. Matt muttered a protest when he felt her slip out of his arms, but she shushed him gently.

'It's OK. I've got to get going, but you haven't,' she whispered. 'Stay in bed. Rest. Enjoy.'

'Can't enjoy without you,' he mumbled, reaching for her with his eyes still closed. But Lesley just laughed softly and dodged his arms, dashing for the bathroom before she gave in to the very real temptation to crawl back into bed beside him.

Once she got downstairs to the workshop area, the demands of the conference took over. It was informative, exciting and exhausting. And Lesley got caught up in it, going from workshop to workshop taking reams of notes, making marginal addenda to various handouts, getting more and better ideas about how to serve the children of her small Maine school district.

She was surprised when Matt caught her between workshops mid-morning and kissed her soundly in front of fifty of her colleagues, making her embarrassed and most of them frankly envious. But, before she could do any more than blush, he winked and said, 'Don't worry. I won't stay around and distract you, much as I'd like to. But I'll be back to hear your talk. When are you on?'

Lesley grimaced. 'Last shot of the day—four o'clock. But you don't have to,' she added quickly. 'Really. It isn't necessary.'

'It is. You're my wife, and I intend to be there.' He gave her another quick kiss and strolled off.

Mary Potter had given her a catch-all title— 'Responsibilities to children'—and the admonition to 'make people think'. Other people had talked about family counselling, contagious diseases, child abuse, sex education—issues of substance. To finish off the day, Mary said, she didn't need any more consciousness-raising.

'I want *conscience*-raising from you,' she had told Lesley when she gave her the topic.

Lesley did her best. But facing a crowd of nearly six hundred nursing professionals was daunting. Knowing that Matthew was out there somewhere in that crowd, she told herself as she walked to the podium, should have made things worse. She should have been more keyed up, more nervous. Oddly though, once she got started, once she found her focus, it wasn't hard at all.

She was talking to a roomful of people, yes. But she was talking about a topic dear to her heart. And in reality it didn't matter how many people were there listening in, she talked only to him.

She summarised in personal terms what earlier speakers had said. She applied it, spoke in specifics, named names and cited situations, expressing as best she could her own world view—a view that said getting involved wherever one was was the right and proper thing to do.

Finally, summing up, she said, 'People—and in the instance I am speaking of here, children—are ultimately what matters. Individuals. Men and women. Boys and girls. They are the ones we care for. They have names, ages, homes, families. They have pasts, and, ultimately, if we care enough, futures.

'We must not jeopardise those futures. We must not take others' lives lightly, use them carelessly, waste them needlessly. Every person we meet, every person whose life touches ours, is important.

'That's what I'm here to remind you about today. It's nothing fancy, nothing difficult. It's simply to say that we must always remember to care. We may not be able to save the world. We may not even be able to understand it.' Her eyes stopped moving now. She had found Matthew's face, and she couldn't look away from it. He was watching her, his dark eyes intent, his jaw tense. And she smiled now, just for him. 'But we can make a difference. The most important thing is to be able to look back and know we did what we could—to be able to live our lives without regrets.'

Lesley was a resounding success. Mary Potter thought so; the president of the regional school nursing association thought so; clearly the mobs of listeners who stopped her to shake her hand and congratulate her thought so. She only hoped Matt agreed.

Her eyes darted about constantly even as she shook hands

and mouthed thank-yous. She craned her neck, trying to spot him over the heads of crowds of milling bystanders. But it wasn't until the throng thinned considerably that she saw him at last, leaning quietly against a wall.

She smiled at him, feeling suddenly awkward and hesitant. He was regarding her gravely, but as she moved towards him he straightened, and when she reached his side he held out an arm to her and pulled her close, hugging her hard against him.

'How was I?' she couldn't help asking.

He looked down at her, smiling almost wryly. 'Hard to live up to,' he said.

Lesley gave him a curious look. 'What?'

He shook his head, smiling still. 'Doesn't matter. You were terrific. Your Mary Potter has invited us to dinner with her. Shall we accept or not?'

Another time she would have said yes. Mary was charming and good company. But not tonight. Lesley was still charged up, high on the adrenalin from her speech and even higher on her love for Matt. She didn't want distractions now.

'I'd rather it'd be just us,' she said. 'Alone.'

'Me too.'

Mary understood. She would have had to be blind not to. 'Don't worry about it. Enjoy yourselves,' she told them. 'We'll get together another time. And thanks again, Lesley. You were superb.'

Lesley beamed. She couldn't stop beaming. She hooked her arm through Matt's and floated down in the elevator, through the lobby and out of the door.

If their first evening in Boston had been marvellous, this one was enchanted. They walked through the Boston Public Garden, took a ride on one of the swan boats, then ambled through the Beacon Hill area, choosing a tiny Italian restaurant for supper simply because it seemed to be overflowing with the enthusiasm for life that they both felt.

Walking back to the hotel across the Public Garden, they encountered a wedding in progress—a radiant bride, a handsome young groom, family and friends and complete strangers, all solemn participants or witnesses to the beginning of a commitment for life.

Lesley couldn't help it. She started to cry.

'Hey, I thought you'd decided that marriage wasn't that bad.' Matt pulled out a handkerchief and wiped her cheeks, smiling down at her tenderly, kissing her lightly.

'Not bad at all,' Lesley sniffed. 'Good. Beautiful, in fact.' She reached up and returned his kiss. 'The wedding just reminded me, made me aware of the promise. I'm just so glad that it's all worked out.'

Matt stopped and took her in his arms. 'Has it?' he asked her, his tone serious.

'Oh, yes.' She linked her fingers with his and gave him her heart with her eyes. 'I have no more doubts.'

It really was the second honeymoon that Lesley hadn't thought she would ever see. Mary Potter had spread the word, and Lesley and Matt were treated to smiles and nudges, but no one from the conference interrupted their time together. Harry didn't call with any emergencies befalling the children. And no one called for Matt to fly off to Biafra or Bangladesh.

Not that he would have gone. People came first with Matt Colter. Lesley understood that now.

Still, she wouldn't have been human if she hadn't felt a momentary qualm when they drove into the driveway Sunday afternoon and a tall, willowy blonde woman was sitting on the porch talking to Harry and the kids. She stood up and waved when Matt pulled the car to a halt.

It was Becca Walsh.

Lesley stiffened. Then mentally she shook herself. Stop

it, she told herself. There's nothing to worry about.

And there wasn't, she was certain. After a weekend like the one they had just spent together, no story on earth was going to come between them now.

She glanced at Matt to gauge his reaction, and found it even more reassuring. He was ignoring Becca totally, getting out of the car and greeting the kids who had run to meet them. He tousled Teddy's hair and gave the boy a hug with one arm, while with his other he scooped up Rita.

Only when he had reached the porch itself and there was no way to avoid her without being downright rude did he acknowledge Becca.

'To what do we owe the privilege?' he asked Becca, giving her a casual, almost perfunctory smile. 'You're a long way from home.'

'I wouldn't be if it weren't necessary,' she said briskly. She was balancing a cup of coffee that Uncle Harry had obviously made for her, and she looked as uncomfortable and out of place here making small talk on a rural Maine doorstep as she used to make Lesley feel wherever she found her.

She also looked as though she'd had been there quite a while. Lesley wondered how long, but almost immediately Becca told them.

'I called as soon as I got the news. He——' she nodded at Harry '—said you were out of town and wouldn't be back till this afternoon. I got here right after lunch,' she complained. 'I thought you'd be back sooner.'

'We were down in Boston,' Matt said easily. He flipped through the letters on the table, barely glancing at Becca.

'Boston?' Becca practically shrieked. 'I drove up from there.' She looked accusingly at Harry. 'Why didn't you tell me?'

Harry gave her a gentle smile. 'Some things can wait.'

'Not this,' Becca snapped.

'What's new?' Matt asked Teddy, deliberately ignoring her.

'I finished the new rocket,' Teddy told him. 'You wanta see it?'

'Sure.'

'Matt, I *need* to talk to you.' Becca set the cup and saucer on the porch railing with a decided clatter. 'Now.'

Matt looked at Lesley, his expression wary. She gave him a reassuring smile.

'Come on, Teddy,' Lesley said, revelling in her new-born security. 'You can show me the rocket.' She gave Becca a generous smile. 'Take your time,' she said.

She went out to the garage with Teddy and got a far more detailed explanation of the ins and outs of rocketry than she had ever hoped to get. But she didn't mind. In fact, she was pleased. He was so capable, so positive. He fairly glowed with confidence. And a lot of the credit, she knew, went to Matt.

He had been every bit as good a father to Teddy as she could ever have wanted. He had spent time with him, taught him, played with him, loved him. She leaned against the workbench and listened with half an ear while Teddy went on about the principles of rocket flight, while in her mind she thanked God for giving her the good sense to try to trust Matt again, to scrape up the courage to give him another chance.

'We can shoot it off tonight,' Teddy told her. 'As soon as that lady leaves. Think she's gone yet?' he asked hopefully.

He had barely got the words out of his mouth when Lesley heard a car start. She peeped out of the window and saw Becca's blue Mercedes glide down the drive. How many times had she seen the back of her blonde head driving away with Matt's dark one beside her? Too many, that was certain. But no one rode with Becca today.

'She's gone,' said Lesley, and couldn't contain her smile.

Teddy let out a whoop. 'Great! I'll get 'im.' He was already heading for the door.

'After supper.' Lesley followed him back towards the house.

'But——'

'After supper,' she repeated firmly. 'We'll have more time.'

Teddy looked disgruntled, but gave in. 'Then I'll get everything ready,' he said.

'Do that.' Lesley gave him a smile. And she would find Matt, wrap her arms around him and tell him again how glad she was to be his wife.

Only Uncle Harry was in the kitchen. 'Had a good weekend, did you?'

'Marvellous. Thanks for keeping the kids.'

'No problem—any time. They were a breeze. Coulda done without Ms Fidget, though.'

Lesley smiled, feeling benevolent. 'Becca? Did she bother you?'

'Only the way an ornery tiger pacin' in your living-room is apt to bother you. Like to wore a hole in the rug, she did. That's why I got her on the porch.'

Lesley grinned. That sounded like Becca. Patience had never been one of her virtues. And she couldn't have been too thrilled at the outcome of her long wait, either.

Poor Becca. Oh, well, maybe she understood how things were now. Maybe she wouldn't come back. Lesley dropped a kiss on the top of Harry's bald head.

'I'll fix supper in a few minutes. I want to find Matt first.'

'Upstairs,' Harry told her. 'Heard him go.'

'Thanks.' Lesley went up them herself, smiling. They had spent very little of the weekend sleeping, and she knew Matt would catch as much as he could now because he wasn't likely to spend tonight sleeping, either. She expected to find him lying face down on the bed, out cold.

He was wide awake and upright, a grim expression on his face, an open duffel bag before him on the bed.

Just like that.

Lesley stared, disbelieving, unwilling to face the evidence before her eyes.

'I'm going,' he said. 'I *have* to.' His fists clenched at his sides, his eyes implored her.

She wavered, torn. 'But . . .'

'You remember when they caught the men responsible, the ones who kidnapped me?'

'Yes.'

'They've caught the other two.'

'So?'

'So . . . I have to go.'

'But why? You didn't go when they caught the first two.'

He shook his head. 'The trial is starting. I have to go.'

'To cover it for the paper, you mean?'

'Yeah, something like that. I said I would.'

Lesley watched him, astonished, dazed. It didn't make sense. He was moving about like a man possessed.

Abruptly he turned away, going to the closet, yanking shirts off the hangers and tossing them into the duffel bag. Then he turned back to catch her glance again, his eyes intent. 'I'm not leaving you, Les. It won't be like last time, I promise. I won't be long. I wouldn't go at all, but . . .'

He didn't say 'but' what. There was no way to explain it. Not that would make sense in the context of everything else that had happened.

What was going on? It didn't make sense. None of it did. It was like a refrain singing over and over in her head. Just hours ago they had been blissfully happy, committed, their arms around each other, their future assured.

Then Becca appeared and the world swung upside-down.

What had Becca said that no one else had thought of saying? What method of persuasion had worked for her that had failed for everyone else?

Matt tossed a couple of ties in on top of the shirts. Lesley stared at him, her mind whirling, spinning with images of nights in Boston and days by the sea, with memories of other summonses and other responses, of a marriage lost and a marriage found. And she knew—she *knew*—that, Becca or no Becca, trial or no trial, she wasn't letting him go again.

She brushed past him and reached into the bottom of the closet, hauling out the battered old suitcase she had lugged to Colombia and back again. She thumped it on the bed and flipped it open. Then she went to her dresser and opened the top drawer.

Matt paused in his own ransacking. 'What are you doing?'

'Packing.' She laid in a supply of underwear.

'Packing? For what?'

She tossed in stockings. 'I'm coming too.'

'Like hell!'

She looked up and met his gaze fiercely, astonished at how pale he suddenly seemed. 'I want to,' she told him stubbornly, though a wave of doubt washed over her at the sight of his face. Where the hell was his enthusiasm? Was this the man who had said not long ago that he never wanted to be parted from her again?

'It's crazy,' he said gruffly.

'You're my husband. I want to be with you.' She echoed his words to her when he'd told her he fully intended to listen to her speech. She saw that he remembered. His jaw tightened and a nerve ticked in his cheek.

'Come on, Les,' he argued. 'Be reasonable.'

'I am reasonable. What's unreasonable about coming along?'

'It's dangerous.'

'I'll risk it.'

'I don't want you to risk it! I want you here, safe. I don't want my wife taken hostage and——'

'I won't be taken hostage. I imagine the security surrounding this trial will be something to behold. And if I'm with you, I can't think of any place safer.'

'No.' He was taking things back out of her suitcase as fast as she could put them in. 'It's insane. You have to be here.'

'Why?'

'The kids.'

'They have Harry.'

'Harry's an old man.'

'Harry just took them for an entire weekend and said he'd do it again any time.'

'But not while you go gallivanting all over the world,' Matt protested, stuffing her stockings back in her drawer.

'I'm not gallivanting,' said Lesley, taking them out again and laying them in a suitcase. 'I am accompanying my husband.'

Matt closed his eyes and clenched his fists. 'No.'

'Are you saying you don't want me?' She rounded on him, planting herself squarely in front of him, lifting her chin.

'No, of course I'm not saying that!'

'Then what are you saying?'

'I'm saying . . . I'm saying . . .' But he seemed unable to say anything. He raked fingers through dishevelled hair. 'You don't understand,' he muttered.

'So make me understand.'

'I can't.' Lesley saw his jaw working, his fists clenched and unclenched.

'Look,' he said desperately, 'I won't be long. I'll come right back. It's not a big deal.'

'It's a big deal to me,' Lesley said firmly. She took his hand and held it, stroking it, trying desperately to get through to him, not understanding why things were suddenly falling apart. 'Listen to me. We've been through a lot together, Matt. But we've been through more apart. If we're going to make a go of this, I have to be a part of your life. Just as you had to be there for me this weekend, I have to know what happens to you, don't you see? You can't protect me all the time. I don't want you to.'

He looked at her, anguished. She wrapped her arms around him, hugging him close. For a long moment she could feel him resisting, tensing, willing himself to pull away from her. And then resistance faded, and his arms locked around her. He kissed her long and hard, his tongue seeking hers, his body pressing against hers with a desperation she didn't understand.

Then he sighed and set her away from him. 'All right,' he said. 'We'll leave in the morning.'

Lesley smiled heavenward, thanking God for favours large and small, but mostly for the fact that Matt had truly changed. He was going to take her with him.

When she woke up in the morning, he was gone.

CHAPTER ELEVEN

OF COURSE, he might have been in the bath or downstairs having breakfast with Harry and the children, but somehow Lesley knew he wasn't.

One look around her told her that.

Their gear had been lined up next to the door when they went to bed last night, and, while her suitcase was exactly where she had left it, Matt's dirty green duffel bag was gone.

She scrambled out of bed, desperate, frantic. He wouldn't do this! Couldn't do this! Not now.

Maybe he was still downstairs. Maybe he hadn't really left yet. But then she saw the clock. Eight-forty-five. 'The flight leaves at nine. Be at Logan by eight,' Becca had said, 'and you can be on it.'

Lesley knew he was.

There was still fifteen minutes. She could call. Ring the airline. Have him paged.

And, if he answered, what would she say?

She sagged on to the bed and buried her face in her hands. Then she looked up and wiped her eyes and tried to think what to do next.

That was when she saw the note.

It was stuck in the loop of her suitcase handle, written on a scrap of notebook paper. 'Les,' it said, 'I'm sorry. I love you. I'll be back. Matt.'

What did it mean? What did he mean? If he loved her, why in heaven's name had he gone without her? Nothing made sense. In her mind she played back everything that had happened yesterday, trying to figure out why. Why had he agreed to take her, then left her sleeping? What had changed his mind?

The job?

Becca?

Unfinished business?

All of the above?

She couldn't reason. She couldn't even make an educated guess. The only thing she could do was act.

Batar was dry, dusty, smelly, alien and unbelievably hot—everything, in fact, that Maine was not. It should have given Lesley second thoughts.

It didn't. Though it wasn't the first to have tried.

Harry said she was crazy. 'Good Godfrey, girl!' he had bellowed when she'd come downstairs and announced her intention of following Matt. 'You don't want to go gallivantin' around Batar! That's *the* boiling-point of the world's hotspots, for crying out loud! He was smart to leave you home.'

No, he wasn't, Lesley thought. 'I'm going,' she said. 'If you won't watch the kids, I'll find someone who will.'

Harry, still grumbling, acquiesced. 'You'll need a visa,' he reminded her dampeningly. 'And probably shots.'

Lesley didn't care if they punched her full of holes. She was going after him. 'I'll take care of it.' She was already heading towards the phone as she spoke.

Her father-in-law was even less encouraging when she called to ask him help her secure a visa.

'No place for a girl like you,' he had said in uncompromising tones. 'Stay at home and knit sweaters.'

'I don't knit,' Lesley told him flatly. 'And I'm going whether you help me or not. He's there, being your kind of hero, though lord knows why, and I intend to be there too. He needs me.'

She didn't know why she believed that, given the way he

had run out on her. But somehow—for some reason—she was sure he did. This time was not going to be like all those other times when he had left her. For whatever reason he had gone, he wasn't the same man who had left her before. And she wasn't the same woman. She was no longer afraid that history would repeat itself, the way it had done with her parents. She wouldn't let it.

She was going after him.

Neither Uncle Harry, nor Hamilton Colter nor the U.S. government was going to stop her.

Fifty-nine hours after she awoke to find Matt gone, she was flagging down a cab in Batar.

'Where to go, miss?' The young moustachioed Arab driver asked her.

Lesley consulted a scrap of paper covered with scribbled information gleaned from a hurried telephone chat with a *WorldView* secretary. 'The Royal Palm Hotel?'

He nodded, took her bag and held the door for her, slamming it once she had tucked herself in. Then, before she could even get her bearings, he shot out into traffic.

Batar was a dizzying blend of medieval and twentieth century, of East and West, Moslem and Christian. Skyscrapers and hovels coexisted. Donkeys ran loose alongside Mercedes in the streets. But Lesley noted only half of it. Her mind was preoccupied with Matt. Where was he? What was he doing? And, most important, what had driven him to leave without her?

The Royal Palm was as lavish and cool as the rest of Batar was poor and hot. Bedraggled and exhausted, Lesley stood for a moment in the oasis of a lobby, sucking in the air-conditioned moist air. Then, squaring her shoulders, she picked up her suitcase and marched to the desk. A good offence was her best plan, she reminded herself. A good offence was what they would get.

'Good morning,' she said to the desk clerk. 'I am Mrs Matthew Colter. My husband was expecting me to join him here.' Not precisely a lie. Once upon a time he had assured her she would be coming with him.

'Ah, Mrs Colter, yes.' The desk clerk gave her a wide smile.

Lesley breathed a sigh of relief. He was here!

The clerk consulted his registration list, then frowned. 'Only a single room. Mr Colter did not mention . . .' Suspicious brown eyes flicked up to study her closely.

She wasn't going to lose Matt now. Lesley whipped out her passport, waving it under the clerk's nose. 'My visa had not arrived by the time he had to leave. As you can see, now it has.'

Visa and passport examined, the smile returned. 'Ah, yes. Right this way, Mrs Colter, if you please.' He beckoned to a bellhop. 'Show Mrs Colter to Room 812.'

He did, knocking, and when he got no answer, unlocking the door for her, then handing her the key. Filled with trepidation, Lesley went in.

No one was there.

She sagged against the door, nerveless fingers letting slip the suitcase in her hand.

Get to the airport, she had told herself. Then get to London, to Athens, to Batar. And, once in Batar, the Royal Palm.

She didn't know where to go from here.

She would have dearly loved to flop right down on the king-size bed and sleep for hours. She couldn't.

If in London and New York concierges knew how to get theatre tickets and where the best restaurants were, surely here they would know where internationally known trials were going on? She had to find the concierge.

Taking only a few moments, she splashed water on her face, then changed her dress to one she hadn't slept in, and went back downstairs.

'Trial?' The concierge shook his head at her question. 'For the terrorists, you mean?' When Lesley nodded, he shook his head again. 'Not yet.'

'What do you mean, not yet?'

'Don't start yet. Today Wednesday. Start Saturday.'

'Saturday?'

He nodded again. 'Saturday.'

She got the picture. Batar was not a part of the Western world. Fair enough. But then, where was Matt?

'I'm looking for Matt Colter. Do you know him?'

The man grinned widely. 'Everybody know Colter. Hero.'

His reputation had obviously not abated, then. 'Do you know where he went?'

The man shook his head sorrowfully. 'He leave with tall lady.'

'Blonde?' Lesley guessed. 'Yellow hair?' she added when he looked as if his English didn't extend that far.

'Yes, yes.'

Becca, no doubt. Lesley pushed the thought right out of her head. 'Where's the trial going to be held?'

'Not til Saturday.'

'I understand. But *where* on Saturday?'

'Big white building near mosque. Look—I show you.' He led her out of the building into a wall of heat that nearly knocked her down. 'You see?' He pointed down the road and Lesley saw a minaret in the distance.

She had no way of knowing if Matt was there. But she had no other place to go.

'Thank you,' she said, and began walking.

It took nearly half an hour. Another time she would have spent three or four hours just absorbing everything she saw along the way. Now she hurried, driven by the same compelling need to find him that had been driving her for the last three days.

And it looked as if she had finally succeeded, for as she was going in Becca was coming out.

The blonde woman stopped dead and stared at her. 'You!'

Lesley, sweaty and exhausted, simply nodded and continued up the steps.

Becca grabbed her arm. 'You can't go in there!'

Lesley pulled away. 'Why ever not?'

'It's private. It's illegal. It's . . .'

'Is Matt in there?' Lesley asked.

The answer was obvious before Becca even reluctantly nodded her head.

'Then get out of my way.' And she pushed past Becca up the steps.

'You can't,' Becca was muttering. 'You can't!' And, all the while she was saying it, she was backing up as Lesley walked, instinctively and unknowingly showing her right where to go. She stopped in front of a wide set of double doors and planted her feet firmly on the marble floor.

Behind the doors, Lesley could hear chairs shifting, the murmur of one voice, then another. 'The trial isn't until Saturday, they said.'

'That's right.'

'So what's going on in there?'

'A hearing,' Becca said.

'Matt's covering it?'

Becca looked her right in the eyes, her gaze probing, intent. 'You really love him, don't you?' she asked Lesley. 'You must, to come all this way.'

'Yes.'

Becca closed her eyes momentarily, then seemed to make up her mind. 'All right,' she said. 'Matt's part of it. He's the reason they're there.' She stepped aside and let Lesley in.

It was a courtroom, spacious, high-ceilinged, with white walls and dark institutional furniture. At the far end, on a raised platform, three men—one in a business suit, two in traditional Arab robes—sat facing her. Judges. She could tell just by looking at them. They looked at Lesley momentarily when she came in. So did a young man—no more than a boy, really, who was sitting by himself off the platform to the judges' left.

No one else turned around. She glanced over the few heads in front of her, all of whom sat facing the judges. She spotted Matt at once. He was sitting up ramrod-straight in a chair in the front row. Even as she spied him, a man stood and spoke to him, 'You may come forward now, Mr Colter, if you please.'

Matt stood, hesitated for just a moment, then squared his shoulders and walked up to take a chair to the right of the judges.

If her courtroom knowledge extended to the Middle East, Lesley guessed it was comparable to the witness stand. Hurriedly she slipped into one of the chairs beside the aisle.

'Mr Colter, you have asked for this hearing to explain why you believe some charges should be dropped,' one of the judges said in gravelly British-accented tones. 'Is that correct?'

Lesley's fingers knotted. Dropped? Which ones? Why?

She glanced at the boy again. Was he the one Becca had referred to—the terrorist who was only a kid? He looked barely older than Teddy.

Was that why Matt had come? To help him?

Lesley shifted in her chair, leaning forward, wanting to know more, watching Matt, her gaze intent, his desertion of her forgotten. Her chair squeaked and Matt looked up.

He saw her then and went absolutely white.

'Mr Colter?' the judge prodded.

Matt blinked, swallowed, licked his lips. 'What?' His

voice was a hoarse croak.

'I said, you have asked us for a special hearing to explain why charges against Ali ben Rashad should be dropped, is that true?'

Matt's eyes met Lesley's across the courtroom. They were bleak and sleepless and full of pain. He shut them, then swallowed. 'Yes.'

'Proceed, then.'

Reluctantly, painfully he did. In a ragged voice, speaking slowly, he told all about the long days, the interminable nights, the weeks upon weeks when he was isolated, alone.

'Except when they brought me food,' he said. 'They had a boy who brought me food.'

'Ali ben Rashad?' one of the judges asked, his eyes going to where the young man sat, confirming Lesley's suspicions.

But Matt shook his head. 'His brother, Hamid.' He raked his fingers through his hair before he went on. 'I talked to Hamid,' he said slowly. 'He was my link to sanity, I think—young, impressionable, full of dreams.' His voice was scratchy and it wavered as he spoke.

Lesley knew he was reliving it all.

'I used those dreams,' Matt said harshly, looking up. 'Peace. Freedom. An end to poverty. "You can have it all," I told him. "Just help me get out."' His jaw clenched and he stared defiantly at the judges.

'You are saying he is the one who helped you escape?' The judges stared at him owl-eyed.

'One of them. The other was Ali ben Rashad. Hamid shared his dreams with his brother——' Matt's mouth twisted bitterly at the memory '—convinced him well. They timed the escape. They got me the guns. They gave me and the others the freedom they sought.'

'Hamid ben Rashad?' One of the judges frowned. 'But wasn't he the one who——'

'Who was killed,' Matt finished heavily for him.

'Killed trying to stop you,' the judge corrected.

'No. He was killed, all right,' Matt agreed grimly. 'But he was shot while he was trying to escape with us. By whom, I don't know. Their side? Our side? It doesn't matter. At the time, for Ali's safety, because he was still with them, it was better to let people think Hamid had died trying to prevent the escape.' Matt shook his head, then looked out into the distance, speaking heavily and with great pain. 'It isn't true. He was killed for *my* dreams, for *my* freedom. I might as well have pulled the trigger.'

For an eternity no one said a word.

Beyond the walls of the courtroom, the sounds of traffic churned. A horn honked. Inside, someone coughed. A chair scraped. Lesley sat frozen where she was.

At last one of the judges mumbled something to another. They both nodded, then spoke to the third one who concurred.

Finally the gravelly-voiced one spoke. 'We thank you for your testimony, Mr Colter. We shall give it our gravest attention and return a finding forthwith. You are dismissed.'

Looking neither right nor left, Matt stepped down. He walked straight down the aisle towards the chair where Lesley sat. She stared up at him, mesmerised, horrified at the pain she had witnessed. His jaw was clenched, his eyes staring out into some middle distance. His pace slowed only slightly as he came abreast of her. He paused and his eyes shifted, meeting her own.

'So now you know,' he said in a flat, dull tone.

And before she could respond he strode on by and the door swung shut after him.

Stunned, Lesley stared after him. Did he think she condemned him, for heaven's sake? Did he think she would blame him for Hamid ben Rashad's unfortunate death?

Obviously he did.

'Matt!' She leaped up, almost kicking over the chair in her dash to catch up with him. But he was gone.

She flew down the steps to the street, her eyes flickering back and forth, searching out Western business suits and Matt's rumpled hair. He wasn't there.

Where would he have gone?

The hotel. And then the airport.

Lesley started to run.

So she was going to end up like her mother, after all.

Worse, in fact. Because, if Madge spent her life waiting for Jack, at least now and then he came.

Lesley had beaten Matt back to the hotel. Had beaten him by hours—fifteen, in fact.

And still he hadn't come.

How long was she going to wait? How long until she could admit to herself that he wasn't coming at all? How long until she accepted the fact that he had simply grabbed the first flight out and chalked up his dirty green duffel bag as not worth bothering about?

Lesley sighed, aching, loving him more than she ever had, and afraid she would never be able to find him now and tell him so.

It was past three in the morning when the key turned in the lock. She jerked up in the armchair where she'd sat dozing in the darkness, groping for coherence, settling for vision. Then the light flicked on and suddenly she didn't even have that.

'Lesley?'

The one word was so stark and pain-filled that it hurt her just to hear it. When her eyes finally began to adjust to the light, she saw him clearly. He stood just inside the door shaking his head as if he didn't believe he was seeing her, or as if—she thought wryly—he wished he didn't.

He was in his shirtsleeves now, rumpled and half
unbuttoned, his coat flung over his shoulder, his hair
uncombed, his tie askew. A day's worth of stubble darkened
his lean, pale cheeks, and his eyes looked like burned-out
holes. He should have been celebrating the freedom and the
true story of Ali ben Rashad which had come over the
evening news in three languages; instead he looked as if
he'd been dragged through hell.

'What are you doing here?' he asked roughly.

'Waiting for you.'

He shook his head. 'No point.'

Lesley got up and began to walk towards him. 'Why not?'

'You know why not.' He looked past her, his voice gruff.

'No.'

'You heard.'

'I heard how you saved a boy's life.'

'And heard how I killed one.'

She reached out to touch him, to comfort him, but he
jerked away.

'Don't!'

'I love you.'

He shook his head fiercely. 'No!'

'I do.'

'How can you when you know what I did?' he demanded,
his features anguished.

'I love you *because* you did what you did.'

'*Because* of what I did?' He was aghast.

'Not Hamid. You couldn't help that. You aren't God;
you didn't know. You did what you had to do. I love you
because you care. Because you were concerned enough for
Ali to risk everything *you* cared about to come back here
and help him.' She looked up at him, her eyes beseeching.
'Isn't that true, Matt?'

He stared, swallowed. His eyes widened. He didn't speak,
but she knew she was right. She could see it in his eyes.

Though her throat tightened at the sight of that brief flicker of hope, she determinedly went on. 'That's why you left me at home, isn't it?' she asked gently.

She touched his arm, and this time he didn't pull away. 'Because you thought if I ever found out about what happened with Hamid, I . . . I wouldn't love you.'

He swallowed hard, his dark eyes blurring. 'You couldn't. I was sure you couldn't,' he choked at last, running a shaky hand through his hair.

She touched her lips to his. 'But I do.'

'In Boston you said——'

'I love you.'

She put both her arms around him then, drawing him against her, feeling the tension in him, the last vestiges of resistance, of fear, of disbelief.

And then, at last, he believed.

His coat fell to the floor and his arms came around her too. He buried his face against her neck and his breath came in harsh sobs.

'Oh, Les, I love you!' The words seemed wrenched from the depths of his soul. 'I was afraid to come . . . afraid I'd lose you again. Afraid to bring you . . . afraid to leave you . . .'

'I wasn't letting you leave me,' Lesley said, holding him close, stroking his hair. 'And I'm not. Not ever again. Where you go, I go.'

Matt shuddered, then lifted his head and looked at her.

'I mean it. This time our marriage is going to work,' she said firmly.

Their eyes met, locked. 'You think so?' His voice was half wary, half hopeful.

'Don't you?' she asked archly.

'I want it to. Oh, do I want it to!' His tone was fervent. 'It's all I hoped for, all I dreamed about . . . all those months,' he admitted.

Lesley's eyes widened. She touched his cheek wonderingly.

Matt gave her a wistful smile. 'It was you and Hamid who kept me alive. He provided sustenance for the body. You were food for my soul.'

'Oh, Matt!' She started to cry then.

He pulled her down on to the bed so that they lay side by side. One hand, trembling slightly, came up to stroke her cheek. 'I relived every moment of our marriage, every hour. And I realised how few of them we had spent together.' He grimaced. 'You were right with your ultimatum. I should have listened. I just wasn't used to thinking that way. When we got married, I guess I thought I'd just go on doing what I'd been doing, and you'd fit in somehow.' Sighing, he rolled on to his back and hauled her on top of him. 'In some little corner somewhere, doing your own thing. Like my parents.'

'I should have been more tactful. Tried to understand. Tried to compromise,' Lesley told him softly as he continued to stroke her cheek. 'I didn't. All I could think about was my own parents. I kept remembering the way my father was always getting itchy feet and walking out on my mother, and how she wasted away waiting and waiting for him to come back. I couldn't do that. But I shouldn't have given you an ultimatum either. I don't blame you for not wanting to see me after that.'

Matt's hand stopped stroking. 'I always wanted to see you. I didn't think you ever wanted to see me.'

'I came to your office,' Lesley reminded him.

He frowned. 'When?'

'A couple of weeks later, after you came back from Bali. I waited . . .' She smiled ruefully. 'Hoping. But when you didn't come home, I went to see you. To apologise. To try to work things out. You wouldn't see me.'

He stared at her. 'I wouldn't——? I never——'

'Becca said.'

'Becca?' A crease appeared between his brows. 'Becca said I didn't want to see you? When?'

'I don't remember the day. She said you refused to be bothered. And that night you were on your way to Central America somewhere, I think.' She grimaced. 'So I wasn't surprised you didn't want to see me.'

Matt groaned. 'I remember now. Some rush-rush job. A coup or a disaster or some damned thing. Carlisle was yelling in one ear and Becca babbling in the other. Phones ringing, telexes and wire services running. I had to leave that night and I had a thousand things to finish first. I told Becca I wouldn't see anyone.' His eyes met hers. 'I never meant you. I'm sorry.'

'I'm not,' said Lesley.

He blinked. 'Oh?'

'Would it have done any good then? Would we have been able to change, to make things work? I doubt it.'

Matt smiled wryly. 'You mean you think terrorist captivity's been good for me?'

'Harry would say you made the best of a bad job,' she told him, brushing a lock of dark hair off his forehead. 'And he's always said going to Colombia was good for me.'

Matt shook his head. 'When I think about you down there, it scares me to death. A thousand things could have happened to you!'

Lesley touched his cheek. 'Now you know how I felt about you.'

Matt shut his eyes for a moment. 'I see what you mean.' He sighed. 'And I guess some good did come from it. It got us Teddy and Rita. What a surprise they were!'

'I thought you'd be angry about them. You once said you didn't want any kids. I thought, if anything would drive you away, that would.'

'When I was young and stupid,' said Matt frankly, 'I

thought kids would be a millstone around my neck. Hard to be a travellin' man when you've got a lot of moss.' He gave a wry grimace. 'But when you told me about them, I couldn't believe my luck. I thought, God's giving me a second chance. You know, a way to redeem myself for having caused Hamid's death, seeing that these two had a fair shake. It was atonement then, not Teddy and Rita themselves. That was before I got to know them.' He shrugged, embarrassed almost. 'Once I did, I couldn't imagine not being their dad. I love 'em, Les.'

'Oh, Matt!' Lesley hugged him.

'Besides,' he went on, 'I wanted you back, and nothing was going to drive me away. Not the kids, not anything. Not even you saying you were marrying that damned lobsterman.' He glared at her. 'How could you do that to me?'

'I thought you weren't coming back. I thought you didn't want me any more. It had been so long, and he loved me.'

She felt a sudden tension in him. 'Did you love him?'

Lesley shook her head, sitting up and bending over him, resting her hands against his heart. 'Not the way I love you. I'll never be able to love anyone the way I love you, Matt Colter. Once you said I was stuck with you. Well, it works both ways. You're stuck with me. Forever.'

He blinked, tears misting on his lashes as he smiled up at her. 'Thank heaven for that, then,' he muttered, and wrapped her in his arms. 'Think you could convince me a little?'

'Prove it, you mean?' Lesley asked, rubbing her nose against his bristly chin.

'Uh-huh.'

'Only if you will.'

'Oh, I will,' he promised, sliding his hands beneath her shirt. 'As long and as often as you want. Starting now.'

Smiling, thankful, blessed and knowing it, they came

together at last with no barriers between them. They had only love and need and each other.

It was enough.

Harlequin Presents®

Coming Next Month

**In April, Harlequin brings you the
world's most popular romance author**

JANET DAILEY

No Quarter Asked

Out of print since 1974!

After the tragic death of her father, Stacy's world is shattered. She needs to get away by herself to sort things out. She leaves behind her boyfriend, Carter Price, who wants to marry her. However, as soon as she arrives at her rented cabin in Texas, Cord Harris, owner of a large ranch, seems determined to get her to leave. When Stacy has a fall and is injured, Cord reluctantly takes her to his own ranch. Unknown to Stacy, Carter's father has written to Cord and asked him to keep an eye on Stacy and try to convince her to return home. After a few weeks there, in spite of Cord's hateful treatment that involves her working as a ranch hand and the return of Lydia, his ex-fiancée, by the time Carter comes to escort her back, Stacy knows that she is in love with Cord and doesn't want to go.

**Watch for *Fiesta San Antonio* in July and
For Bitter or Worse in September.**

JDA-1

This April, don't miss Harlequin's new Award of
Excellence title from

Harlequin Presents...

CAROLE
MORTIMER

Award of Excellence

elusive as the unicorn

*When Eve Eden discovered that Adam
Gardener, successful art entrepreneur, was
searching for the legendary English artist, The
Unicorn, she nervously shied away. The Unicorn's
true identity hit too close to home....*

*Besides, Eve was rattled by Adam's
mesmerizing presence, especially in the light
of the ridiculous coincidence of their names—
and his determination to take advantage of it!
But Eve was already engaged to marry her
longtime friend, Paul.*

*Yet Eve found herself troubled by the different
choices Adam and Paul presented. If only the
answer to her dilemma didn't keep eluding her....*

HP1258-1